The Ye
Miracle
and Grief

The Year of Miracle and Grief

LEONID BORODIN

QUARTET BOOKS

First published in English in 1984 by
Quartet Books Limited
A member of the Namara Group
27 Goodge Street, London WIT 2LD

Translated from the Russian, *God Chuda i Pechali*,
by Jennifer Bradshaw
Copyright © Possev-Verlag 1984
Translation copyright © Quartet Books 1984

The right of Leonid Borodin to be identified
as the author of this work has been asserted
by him in accordance with the
Copyright, Designs and Patents Act, 1988

A catalogue record for this book
is available from the British Library

ISBN   978 0 7043 7324 2

Typeset by Antony Gray
Printed and bound in Great Britain by
T J International Ltd, Padstow, Cornwall

Prologue

IT IS TWENTY-FIVE YEARS this summer since I gave my word to the old lady Sarma. This has brought a twofold happiness: first, because of the fact that I actually kept my word, something which could easily be understood by anyone who had managed to do so for even half as long; and secondly, because I can at last tell the story which I have had to keep secret all this time.

Though the term of secrecy expired some months ago, it is only now that I have been able to open my notebook and begin writing, full of feelings of timidity and uncertainty. I used to think that when the time came I would immediately in the space of a few days relate everything which happened to me twenty-five years ago, and that I would do this easily and quickly because I have forgotten nothing – not one word, not a whisper, not a passing thought or intention, good or bad. At that time it never even occurred to me to wonder whether people would believe me, since, after all, I had not the slightest intention of telling a harmless and amusing little fairy-tale which would not be worth wasting paper on. In any case, I am no spinner of yarns.

But what happened to me in childhood – whether one sees the event as a whole or as a sum of its parts – in no way coincides with a conventional childhood story, though I am convinced in the depths of my soul that the thing that I shall describe did not happen to me alone. It probably happened to lots of children, only they, too, are perhaps afraid of not being believed, so they keep silent. But then, I suppose, at least *they* will believe me. Perhaps it is for that very reason that after laying down my pen a few times, smoking a couple of cigarettes and pacing the room for a while, I find myself seated once again, opening my note-book, reading through the ten or so lines on the page, and starting once more to write, in the hope of convincing the reader that my story is true. But at this point, I must issue a warning: my story is quite definitely not a fairy-tale and if the reader should suddenly at a certain point catch himself discrediting what I say, then he should either stop reading altogether or else he must summon up the necessary patience to read on without doubting. Then, perhaps, all doubt will be dispelled as often happens when, in order to believe in something out of the ordinary, one has to break through the invisible barriers which, like a wall or a net, serve to impede and confuse the faculties within each one of us of belief and trust. For I have learned from experience that the truth which exists within us is immensely greater than the truth which is revealed to us in the form of rules and laws in this world of ours.

A miracle is something which occurs in spite of and contrary to everything. According to the rules, it does not happen. Consequently, when a miracle does take place, it does so in defiance of the rules.

To those who have never experienced even the most trifling miracle, I can quite easily offer assistance; for there's no need to travel to the ends of the earth in pursuit. All you need to do is to go to the town of Irkutsk, board the Irkutsk – Slyudyanka train and sit on the left-hand side of the carriage facing forwards.

After veering right from Angar, the train runs alongside a

bright mountain stream. Beyond the river, if you look out of the window opposite, you can see the taiga which, to the accustomed eye of the Siberian, does not look as thick as people generally make it out to be. After a while, you will see, outlined to the left on the horizon, the undulating features of the mountains. (Actually they come somewhere between hills and mountains.) But then you will find that this mountainous cluster is also a common sight in Siberia, and after another ten kilometres or so you will almost certainly grow tired of it, all the more so if you have crossed all of Siberia to reach Irkutsk. Then just as you are about to become irretrievably bored, just as sleep is beckoning or you are closing your book and lying back in your seat, sadly resigned to this tedium, then you will be rewarded beyond all expectation. For suddenly the mountains open up; they do not just part, but open up wide in three different dimensions – upwards, outwards, downwards. And all at once something quite remarkable is revealed. It is as if the train you are travelling on is careering along the top edge of a very high mountain, or rather, on the edge of the world itself. Up above you can see the blue of the heavens, and in the distance the infinite horizon adorned by the crooked line of the Khamar-Daban summits. But if you look down you will see a dazzling expanse of blue water speckled with brown crags. It is such a long way off that at the moment you cast your eyes downwards, you forget your precise vantage-point. You could be on an aeroplane, not a train, or orbiting some unknown planet. The clatter of the wheels will subside as will the rocking of the carriage, and you will gradually cease to feel in motion at all. For in comparison with the limitless expanse of the panorama opening up before your eyes, the speed of the train will seem quite insignificant and you will feel as if you are suspended on the brink of a fantastic world. Your thoughts and feelings, like the train, will come to a standstill and your entire being will be transformed at that moment into a sensation of total rapture in the presence of a *miracle*!

Not everything out of the ordinary is miraculous, of course. A miracle is really a moral concept. This can be confirmed providing you are able to tear yourself away from the window at the psychological moment and look to left and right at your fellow travellers, likewise transfixed by the sight. For in their faces you will perceive an expression of openness quite exceptionally kind and sincere. You will then be able to sense that quality, almost intangible, which distinguishes man from every other creature, that which makes him specifically human . . .

The miracle which will be revealed to you if you sit on the left-hand side of the Irkutsk train, facing forwards, is called Lake Baikal, and this lake will be one of the principal heroes of the tale which I am at last ready to begin, now that I have assured the reader of the absolute truth of every word I am about to write.

1

WE WERE TO GO and live in a village on the shores of Lake Baikal where my parents were to teach at the railway school. This rendered us, in effect, railway people and so we were assigned a special goods waggon for the move. Several times before we got under way my father had to rush off on some errand, or people would come to us to check our papers and boxes, after which our waggon was shunted endlessly back and forth. It was only towards evening that we eventually found ourselves in the middle of the convoy of closed and sealed waggons, and well into the night that the thunderous din of some raucous fish porters signalled the fact that we were on our way.

We arrived at Baikal after dark on the third day. I peered through a chink in the door but could see nothing. It was impenetrably dark. But at that first stop I immediately became aware of an unfamiliar sound very near to our waggon. Something large and heavy was breathing half angrily, half threateningly, and these deep breaths emitted a cold draught which made the air quite different from what it had been earlier. For some reason it made me want to inhale deeply all the time and this in turn set my head spinning and chest tightening either from the freshness or the dampness. The aroma which crept out of the darkness did not remind me of anything, but it was so powerful that it suppressed all the other waggon smells and somehow made its own way to the nostrils which in turn opened wide to meet it.

We travelled for some hours along the shore of Lake Baikal, although I had no notion of how we could be doing this and could imagine even less what it looked like. It was pitch-dark when Father announced that we had arrived. It seemed incredible that anyone could have come to meet us in such darkness, but two men got into the waggon, shook hands with my parents, bade them welcome, and me too. They wanted to give me some treat but they searched their pockets and found nothing. They both promised me something for the following day, one to show me a bear-skin, the other to take me ice skating. There were so many new thoughts and impressions to be absorbed that at some point I fell into a sort of trance and I can now hardly remember the distant succession of events, though I do remember how they unloaded the waggon in the dark, carried the things away and, still in the dark, took me off somewhere. But from somewhere I could again hear quite distinctly the rumble of that alien creature breathing, somewhere very near, almost beneath my feet. The coldness which came from the same direction was autumnal, not summer, and it rose in a solid current and brushed my shoulders.

Before going into the house, I remember standing on the first step of the porch, looking up at the sky and feeling horrified: it had been cut off on all sides by great dark hulks. I guessed that these were mountains and that our house stood down below among them. The place we are going to live in is . . . a grave for a thousand elephants! – that is exactly the thought which came into my mind. I was terrified and wanted to go to sleep.

*

Just as in fairy-tales, I woke up in a world absolutely different and new. It was blindingly bright in the room and the first thing I saw was a crooked, warm square of sun hanging on the wall. The room already looked habitable and I was lying, not on the mattress where I had collapsed the night before, but in a bed by the window. The curtains were familiar as was the vase containing flowers on the sill. The great disc of the sun shone in at the window and I could not look out. I tried, by shading my eyes with my hand, to see what there was out there, but it was too bright. Then I remembered that this was not the train but a house which must have a door, beyond which everything would be at hand, for ever. So I pulled on my trousers and shirt, roughly laced my boots and, without yet knowing the layout of the house, threw myself at one of the two doors and landed in the kitchen. Without a word to my mother, without even looking at her or inhaling the delicious smells coming from the stove, I made a full-length dash for the outer door and leapt out on to the porch. The 'grave for a thousand elephants' turned out to be a gigantic ravine where not a thousand, but seemingly a hundred thousand elephants could have been buried. The mountains were much higher than they had seemed the previous night; I could never have imagined anything like them. The front steps looked out on to one side of the ravine and to my right, on the very summit of a mountain, perched on a steep yellow crag, sat the sun, dangling his legs. He looked so comfortable sitting there that you might have thought that in this part of the world he did not cross the sky at all but spent the whole day on his rocky armchair, hiding behind it only at night.

Both sides of the ravine were covered in bushes and,

further on, the birch groves sprang up. Still higher, the pine trees crowded against one another. This, no doubt, was already the taiga. I did not yet know that the bushes were wild rosemary and the pine trees cedars. In fact I knew nothing of my surroundings at all. I just stood there feeling madly excited at the sight of this fantastic scenery, the like of which I had never seen before.

Across the gorge, which seemed to plunge into nothingness, stood another mountain that loomed even larger than the rest. And to the left, along a narrow, stony gully, a little stream came leaping down over the stones towards me. Just as my eyes were getting used to the sight, my ears were filled with the surging sound of this mountain stream, rushing away somewhere behind the house.

Further down the gorge, along the banks of this stream, some houses stood one above the other, flanking a winding road which led to a large two-storey building in the depths of the ravine. I guessed that this was the school.

The left side of the ravine was nearer to our house and once again I looked around, absorbing the whole view from the foot of the mountain to the horizon, which, to my unaccustomed gaze, hung so oddly above my head. At that point I experienced a feeling which I have kept all my life: these mountains are there to be climbed, I thought. I cannot remember how many years ago it was that I climbed a mountain for the last time, but every time I find myself in mountainous country, I measure and assess each crag: here I would catch hold of the overhang, there I would pull myself up, or there I would jump across . . . And every time I come across a seemingly unassailable mountain peak or crag, it disturbs and angers me so much that I can become quite discomposed, although probably for the mountain climber there is no such thing as an unassailable mountain. I was never a professional mountaineer myself and to subjugate a mountain with the help of ropes and other accessories has always seemed to me every bit as sacrilegious as getting up there in a helicopter!

At that time, however, twenty-five years ago, my whole being responded spontaneously to this burning urge to climb. I left the steps at a run and, leaping from rock to rock across the stream, I started to bound up the slope of the ravine. But it was much steeper than it had looked from the porch and after a few steps I was on all fours. Clutching at the grass, the moss and the bushes, I clambered up, not stopping to take breath, but after about fifty metres my lungs gave out. When I stopped, straightened up and turned my face to the gorge, the height at which I found myself so terrified me – especially the sight of the miniature houses – that my short breaths turned into spasms. I began to sway and at that moment, for the first time in my life, I became aware of the contradiction between the soul's endeavour to climb and the body's inclination to fall. I sat down, catching hold of the moss, unable to tear my eyes away from the steep slope below and the solid void before me. In the end I managed to turn away and focus on a new field of vision which, from the porch where I had stood before, had been screened by the house.

There, beyond the upturned triangle of the gorge, the railway line ran along a very high embankment crossing a double-arched bridge that straddled the very mouth of the gorge. This was beautiful, but was as nothing compared with the unbelievable white nothingness which stretched endlessly beyond the railway and the ravine.

In my fifth-year school geography book I had learned

how people in ancient times had imagined the end of the world. I remember a picture of some eccentric character, his head thrust forward, looking beyond the frontiers of the known world into a chaos of discarded, scattered objects. But this struck me as being totally devoid of logic since what sort of world's end could it be which could have something beyond that end? If the end of the world really existed, then it had to look like what I could see here – this endless white nothingness. However, not being as naive as the first men on earth, I soon guessed that what I saw was mist! Usually mist appears in shreds or patches or bands, but here it was a smooth, white, milky substance outlining very distinctly the contours of the ravine's slopes, and everything behind it and as far as the sky itself dissolved into a peace so absolute as to be nothingness itself.

It was just possible to make out traces of the sky where it was still a little blue before it faded slightly and then disappeared completely, mingling with the great expanse behind some imperceptible line of reality.

The nothingness was near at hand. Only seventy metres separated me from the bridge and so, forgetting my fear of heights and sheer drops, I literally leapt down the mountain and though I tumbled, tripped, and was flung to one side and then the other, I did not get a single scratch. It was as if I had flown through the air in a single second and I imagined it to have been one of those rare moments when the soul finds its wings . . .

I ran without stopping along the stony bank of the stream and dashed under the bridge just as the train came past. The clatter of the waggons as they thundered over the bridge was deafening and made me crouch in terror. The concrete columns of the bridge droned and shook and bits fell into the space between the tracks. I craned my neck to see the train flashing by, which somehow made me feel as if I were lying under it, suicidal. The train rumbled away but the bridge still echoed with its rumbling.

I finally came back to earth and rushed out headlong from under the bridge into the embrace of that magical mist. I had run hardly any distance when I suddenly felt a burning sensation on my legs. At first I did not understand what was happening and it was only when I bent over that I saw the water. I stepped back a few paces and looked straight ahead but could still see nothing but white mist all around. Then I crouched down and, with little steps, stole up to the water's edge. It was as smooth and bright as glass. It could deceive the eye, I thought, but not the touch. For when I touched it gently with my fingers, it parted willingly, as if breaking the pretence, and allowed my hand to dip in its wintry cold. But as soon as I removed my hand it reverted to glass.

I sat there for a long time gazing at the pebbles under the glass, pulling one out from time to time, as if to prove that they were as real as they looked. When I looked up the mist had lifted and was now quite far away, and though there still hung an unbroken white curtain across the horizon, the mist was retreating before my very eyes and the vitreous expanse was opening up wider and wider before me, without the slightest movement or wrinkle betraying its real nature. The more the expanse opened out, the more definite became the impression of a vast never-ending sheet of glass that stretched from my feet to the sky, covering the rest of the earth.

But glass is fragile, and since children's natural thirst for knowledge makes them want to verify the quality of objects,

I bent down and picked up a large stone. Though I felt like a delinquent standing before a window on the point of vandalising it, the feeling was none the less irresistible and I swung my arm back and threw the stone as far as I could. There was indeed a sound of breaking glass as the fragments flew upwards, leaving circles of tracks like the grooves in a record. The first, deepest groove reached me and reproach-fully licked my boots which were quite wet enough already. But within a few minutes of my act of vandalism, not a trace of it remained: the glass had recovered its former smoothness as if nothing had happened. If only the windows of houses had the same property, how much happier a boy's childhood would be!

'That's not very far at all!' I heard a girl's voice shout behind me. 'I can get it much further!'

I turned round and saw two little girls, one my age, the other about five years old but an exact copy in miniature of the first. Both were fair-haired, snub-nosed and freckled.

'I can easily throw it further,' the older girl repeated. She picked up a pebble and threw it, as all little girls do, over her head, as if she were catching a fly. Of course, the pebble, being so small, went much further. I could have thrown that sort of stone as far as the mist. But I said nothing.

'Svetka, catch me a fish!' whined the younger girl.

'Oh, give me some peace, can't you?'

'Well, I'll tell Papa you fired caps at the boys!'

Svetka (the name suited her uncommonly well*) looked in alarm first at her sister, then at me, and muttered, 'Oh, you are a sneak! All right, then . . . Just a minute.'

* The name Svetka comes from the Russian word *svet* meaning 'light'. [Tr.]

She tore off her shoes, waded into the water up to her ankles and, eyes downwards, shoulders bent, moved along the water. I walked beside her, amazed that she could bear such cold water on her legs. She tucked up the ends of her dress, sat down on the bank and turned over one stone after another in the water until suddenly she cupped one hand into a boat shape, stood quite still, then slowly lowered it into the water. She slapped the water with her free hand and all of a sudden there was a little fish, blue with yellow fins, squirming in her palm. My astonishment knew no bounds. Ordinary mortals have to sit for hours on the river bank, patiently casting their lines, while this little girl could catch fish quite easily with her bare hands.

'It's a yellow-fin,' Svetka said, noticing my interest.

'Let me see!'

'Give it to me, give it to me!' sniffled her little sister.

'Oh, don't be so greedy! I'll get you another one.'

While I examined the beautiful little fish, Svetka caught another and gave it to her whimpering sister.

'You're with the new schoolteachers, aren't you?'

I nodded.

'And my Papa is the school bursar. He's a hunter. Do you want to see a bear?'

'A bear?'

'Well, the skin. Papa killed a bear in the spring.'

From then on I knew that my whole life in this place would be attended by wonders, and this prediction of endless novelty filled me with a joy, quiet and serene. I followed Svetka home to see the bear-skin with the curiosity of a serious, grown man, not easily surprised, but pleased when he is.

Svetka threw the skin over herself and lurched towards

me, growling. Then I took the skin, put it on and did the same in turn. Nelka, her younger sister, howled and screamed incessantly at us. Svetka, breathless, told me what had happened.

'When they brought in the bear from the taiga, they sat him on the porch as if he were still alive . . . The dogs all ran away, and you should have heard them barking! Papa caught our dog, Sharik, and threw him at the bear. Sharik was so frightened, he left a mess all over the porch!'

I cried with laughter, just as she did, although deep down inside I sympathised completely with that poor Sharik.

Svetka's father came in and turned out to be the same man who had helped us the night before to unload and get our things to the house. He let me hold a gun and a hunting knife and a bullet with a special name, used to shoot bears.

Svetka invited me to go with her that evening to fetch the cows from the drop. It turned out that no one there said 'ravine' or 'canyon' but simply 'drop'. In the morning all the cows were apparently herded into the drop and in the evening their owners went to fetch them and take them home.

When I left Svetka's house I was intercepted by Mother who dragged me home and made me sit down and eat my breakfast. I gulped down the last piece of toast on the porch.

The whole day was spent making new acquaintances and forming impressions. I made friends with Valerka, also the son of a teacher, so I was not alone in my position. This happy discovery was reinforced when Yurka, Valerka's friend, befriended *me*.

I assisted at the explosion of a detonating cartridge. These were used by the railway men to stop or warn trains and consisted of small pots, similar to those used for hand cream or shoe polish, but filled with gunpowder and caps. Stealing these caps from their parents was a popular exploit for the local children. They would put the cap on a large stone under a precipice and, from the safety of a little ridge, they would throw another large stone on top so as to smash it. The resultant explosion sounded like a grenade going off and it was considered most heroic to stand as close as possible when it exploded.

The main topic of conversation among my new friends was the taiga: they talked of hay-making in the taiga, of feeding hay to the cows and goats in the marshes and on the edge of the forest, of the cedars and the places where the wild berries grew.

The most interesting person in the neighbourhood was old Vassina. She was the local witch and all the boys, except Yurka, were afraid of her and seemed to hate her. But she had saved Yurka from the bite of an adder and if anyone started to insult old Vassina, Yurka would frown and say menacingly, 'If anyone touches Vassina, I'll twist his tail!'

To 'twist someone's tail' was the most terrible threat. Almost every family had goats, sometimes as many as ten. In winter the goats ate the hay which had been stored for them, but in summer they would go of their own accord and graze in the mountains and on the crags. The drop behind the village was completely laid out with vegetable gardens; goats and vegetable gardens are like cat and mouse. It was generally agreed, and had been proved in practice, that the only way to teach a goat a lesson was to 'twist its tail'. This meant that once the goat had been caught in the garden the owner would twist the offender's tail as if in a vice until the poor goat's bleating became a desperate howl.

When it was freed the goat would gallop off at full speed into the gorge and often went on screaming for a long time. After climbing on to the nearest crag it would turn its bearded head and look down at its torturer who, returning its gaze in cruel triumph, would nod his head sententiously and say, 'Now just you try climbing down again!'

Yurka enjoyed a great deal of prestige with all the other boys, partly because of his brother, who was a cinema projectionist. It was the greatest honour for anyone to meet Yurka's brother personally, an honour which for some reason Yurka decided to bestow upon me, though I had done nothing as yet to deserve it. He invited me the following day on a fishing trip, which meant that with his brother I would make up the third member of the party, something which obviously made Valerka envy me a good deal. The third in the 'Tarzan' series was expected any day now and the seats being more expensive than usual, there was not even any point in asking one's parents for the money.

The sun had taken all day to go round the ravine and towards evening he sat down on another crag and looked as if he had no intention of moving any further. It got colder towards evening and before going to the pastures with Svetka to get the cows, I ran home where I was once again forced to have something to eat. Then I put on my jacket and went out.

We walked through the village as far as the school, after which the road looped round and became much narrower and stonier. The drop was not more than a hundred metres at its widest point and it, too, gradually tapered as we left the village behind. Everywhere we looked, over both sides of the road, vegetable gardens clung to the slope, and the road often meandered through the garden fences.

As I looked out from the porch that morning I had noticed a high crag which seemed both to block off the entrance to the ravine and to tower above it. The further we got from the village, the more swiftly and impetuously did we seem to be approaching it. It was a most unusual crag which grew and grew before our eyes till they were riveted to it. There were no trees on it except for one on its very peak, near the sky – a pine tree with four branches in all. The two top ones were a little smaller and reached up towards the heavens, while the other two pointed down along the trunk. Although this pine was very far away and very high up, it stood out against the backdrop of the sky, illuminated by the setting sun, and you could see its trunk and branches in every detail. The crag itself looked like a ruined castle because all around it lay enormous stones of various shapes; some looked like houses but there was not a single shrub growing near them.

Svetka noticed me staring at it. 'That's Dead Man's Crag. That's what it's called and you mustn't ever climb it. It's slippery all over. And look how many stones there are! They're always falling down. Last year Lyaskin's cow went up there and the stones killed her.'

We had already got quite close to Dead Man's Crag. The sun was no longer on our backs but it was still in the sky. With that sky as a backcloth the crag seemed sinister and evil, as if it were deliberately holding on to some terrible secret . . .

Everyone knows that if you look out of a dark room through a bright window and then close your eyes, you will still see behind your closed eyes the silhouette of the window with its frame and even its ventilation point, if it has one.

We both stopped and while Svetka looked about her, I stared at the pine on the crag. I looked hard, then closed my eyes. According to the rules the silhouette of the pine and its four branches should have remained behind my closed eyes. But what I had just seen instead forced me to open my eyes at once. The look on my face at that moment must have been one of extreme fear because Svetka looked at me, then at the crag, and said, 'It's terrifying, isn't it?'

I nodded in agreement but quickly thought better of it and started to shake my head. 'No, it's really nothing out of the ordinary.' But my voice betrayed me and Svetka did not believe me.

The road forks to left and right at Dead Man's Crag, both halves disappearing into wooded hollows where little paths merged with them. In one of these dips the village cows would be grazing, but Svetka could not quite decide which way to go. Behind us, along the road, villagers were coming like us to search for their cows and the ravine was filled with the sound of voices, especially children's.

'Over there!' cried Svetka, indicating a hollow to the right. I saw nothing of course and could not even for a second bring myself to look in the required direction, transfixed as I was by Dead Man's Crag. I was gathering up the courage to repeat the experiment with the silhouette. After all it could be nothing more than an optical illusion. Sure enough, it was an illusion – or so I told myself as I opened my eyes too quickly to prevent a repetition . . .

Svetka pulled at my arm. 'Let's go!'

I remained, rooted to the spot. 'You go on . . . I'll wait for you here.'

'He's scared! He's scared!' exclaimed Svetka, jumping up and down.

'I'll wait here,' I repeated sullenly, without taking my eyes off Dead Man's Crag.

'Well, all right then, you wait!' shouted Svetka as she skipped away to where the tinkle of cowbells could now be heard only faintly, for the cows, knowing what was expected of them, had wandered off in the right direction.

I looked back to see if I would be able to do what I wanted while the villagers were still approaching. Satisfied that I had enough time, I glanced again at the crag and its pine. Then I fixed my eyes on it for a long time till they hurt, at which point I closed them. The same thing happened, and though I wanted to open my eyes again my lids were so tightly closed that they refused to obey me. A strange cold feeling entered my heart and penetrated my body down to my feet and it was there, in my boots, that I felt terror. When I eventually managed to open my eyes everything was in its usual place – an ordinary crag with an ordinary pine on top, but I could no longer believe what my eyes saw, only what they did not see. I turned on my heels and fled from the crag, almost knocking over some of the villagers coming to get their cows. They looked at me in surprise and probably turned round to stare as I ran off.

Yurka stopped me by the school. 'What's up with you?'

'Nothing,' I replied, hardly able to catch my breath.

'Let's go and get the cows together.'

I shook my head. 'I've got to go home.'

'Are you coming on the fishing trip?'

'Yes,' I shouted, already running off.

I ran all the way home and into the porch where I coughed and spluttered for a long time, my head spinning. When I finally recovered I was amazed and wondered just what I had fled from. What was it I imagined I had seen? And was I not an idiot to have left Svetka? She would surely start looking for me. What a fool I was! What a fool!

Mother and Father were at home. 'You've had a good run, haven't you! Well, do you like it here?' I spent a long time telling them my impressions and talked and talked throughout supper. Only when I referred to the crag did I feel again something resembling that cold sensation, and I suddenly felt I wanted to go straight to bed. Before going to sleep, however, I went out on the porch and looked for a while in the direction of Dead Man's Crag which, though not visible in the darkness, still gave out a tremor of fear which crept out of the night and entered my soul. It was probably nothing more than the cool evening breeze off the mountains, or the joy born of a new life where each new happiness can cause anxiety in case the following morning turns out to be less wonderful than the day just gone.

It seemed as if I had just fallen asleep when Mama shook me by the shoulder and ruffled my hair: 'Time to get up! They've come to get you for the fishing trip.' I would never before willingly have risen so early but here, even though I was not yet properly awake, I jumped out of bed and hurriedly began to dress. Lake Baikal was transformed. It was impossible to believe that yesterday it had been a bright smooth surface without a single ripple from shore to infinity. Was it possible that the same expanse should now resemble the sea? That the lightest wind should chase ripples across the water and that, when the wind stopped, the ripples should keep going in the same direction like dark-blue arrows? Well, it certainly was like that today. The whole lake was dark blue and even darker blue ripples scudded all over its surface from north to south. That at least was how it appeared when we reached the shore.

'It'll be the Kultuk today. That's good,' said Yurka, and his brother from the cinema nodded in agreement. We walked along the edge of the railway line and as we went Yurka told me a great deal about Lake Baikal, all the things, he said, which everyone ought to know, even if he lived in Moscow, because there was nowhere like Lake Baikal and never would be.

'It'll be the Kultuk today,' Yurka repeated, and by then I knew that this was the name of a wave which would soon be coming up from the south and would provide good fishing since it would carry the fish right up to the shore – grayling in particular. There were large fish that lived in the deep and came to shore only during a swell. At such times, the waves would beat down on the shore and dislodge from under the rocks the roe of the gobius, that same fish which Svetka had caught in her hand. The female gobius would swim under a stone, float on the bottom, turn herself upside down and deposit the roe on the underside of the stone. She did this close to the shore to prevent larger fish eating it. The fishermen collected this roe, pickled it, pressed it and then used it as bait to catch the grayling. This roe was not like caviar, nor was it good to eat, owing to its bitter taste.

We walked and walked. I could not understand why we had to go so far since there was water all around and the shore looked uniformly stony wherever we passed. The opposite shore was not visible and we could see only thick grey and white clouds which lay on the water itself, or at least that is how it seemed. On our shore the water started to splash up, which was puzzling since there were no waves as such, only one dark-blue ripple sliding backwards and forwards, first towards the shore, then away from it. But at times the whole surface became covered in these dark ripples, nearer dark grey than blue, almost black, then the wind would die down and the water would again turn blue. I wanted it to stay that colour but the sky, too, just like the water, seemed undecided, as if not knowing which colour to assume that morning. One moment it would be blue, the next it would become covered in grey patches which blended with the clouds on the horizon.

A train flew past us as we stood on the very edge of the track so that we could have reached out and touched the waggons which roared as they flashed by. The railway line followed a narrow, stony strip of land by the lake, beneath an overhang of cliffs which seemed to have been chiselled by hand. While the train kept us on the edge of the embankment, I stared upwards, trying to imagine how high the cliffs reached. It seemed as if they must be several thousands of metres, as the very top was concealed by a jutting rock that hung over the railway track.

After walking on a little we went down a narrow gully from the embankment to the shore itself, which was covered with enormous rocks. There we found two railway sleepers, wedged in the bank between boulders and sticking out of the water. This place was called the pit because of a hole left by a falling rock. The pit without a doubt was nine or ten metres deep and it was here that the grayling came during the swell, swimming close to the shore. It was the best place of all to catch fish.

When we got down to the water the swell had already begun, though the waves were not very high and rose up one behind the other, quietly and unhurriedly, not in straight formation but sideways. A wave would first splash its brow on to the shore, as if greeting it warmly, and then its crest, seeing the end was near, would flop down on the ground at our feet, just as the next wave was already falling on to the rocks, showering them with handfuls of bright spray.

Yurka and his brother retrieved their enormous fishing rods, hidden among the rocks from their last trip. Vitya's was ten metres while Yurka's measured seven and a half metres, both consisting of two parts joined together by a metal tube. They both threw a bag of roe-bait over their shoulders, lifted up their fishing rods and clambered up on to the narrow, sodden sleepers on which it would have been quite difficult enough to keep their balance without the rods. They put the bait on their hooks and cast their lines as far as they could. They propped the rods up against their thighs and froze in that position, fixing their gaze on the blue-feathered floats which bobbed about on the water, bending backwards and forwards. Several times I jumped up and cried out, thinking the fish had bitten, but the boys just stood there like stone statues without the slightest movement, almost as if they had forgotten why they had come there.

The grayling is a noble fish, having nothing in common with the perch or carp who, like fools, always swallow down the bait immediately and then tug at the float and line as if to announce to the fisherman that his job is over and it only remains for him to pull in his line from the water. But the grayling first tries to knock the bait off the hook with its tail and only then, if he is very hungry, will he carefully try to get it into his mouth. As he does this, the float trembles very slightly and you have to be able to hook him at that precise moment. Moreover, you must hook him gently so as not to tear his mouth and before he has time to let go of the bait – all this with a nine-metre fishing rod in your hands and a line that has plunged eight metres into the deep.

And then there is the position into which the fisherman freezes for the catch: the blunt end of the rod is held somehow against his thigh, the sharp end hovers some way above the float; his left hand is on his left thigh and his whole body is tilted back slightly. There is something in his bearing which suggests not only a readiness to pounce, but a distinctive daring, a quiet serenity, even a little carelessness and a look of utter impassivity on his face.

Although the sleepers were wedged tightly against the bank, they still sprang back underfoot as the waves thrust against the fishermen's legs. If a fish were to bite, they would have to hook it, pull it in, catch the grayling with the left hand while holding the rod tight to their bodies with the right, take the fish off the hook, throw it in the bag or on to the shore, put on some more bait and once again swing those enormous rods and cast their lines – all this without losing their balance, or slipping or dropping their rods into the water. Moreover, the grayling is a nervous creature and the roe is barely attached to the hook, so if the fishermen make an unsuccessful strike, the bait comes off and the whole operation must begin again.

I observed my friends for about ten minutes and my admiration was boundless. After another few minutes, however, I dozed off, propped up against a rock. I dreamed that a giant fish leapt out at me from among the rocks, opened its mouth wide and bellowed: 'You've slept through it all, fisherman!' and went off cackling. Exactly at that moment something hit me in the stomach. I jumped up and saw a fish at my feet. Yurka and Vitya stood by their catch, laughing: 'You've slept through it all, fisherman!' shouted Yurka. 'Go and gather some wood and light a fire. We'll cook it.' Vitya showed me where I could collect the wood. While I lit the fire eight more fish were thrown, one after the other, on to the shore. They were large ones, weighing at least two pounds each, according to Vitya.

When the fish stopped biting they came back to the shore, put down their rods on the rocks and began cooking the fish in a way quite new to me. The fish were wrapped in newspaper and put on the fire, right on to the burning cinders. When they were removed the paper was only lightly yellowed and you could still make out letters in places. The fish itself turned out to be excellently cooked and needed only a little salt.

While the fish cooked and while we ate and waited for another swell, Vitya told me all about Lake Baikal. He told me of the two great waves, the Kultuk and the Barguzin, and of the Sarma, a wind that tore trees from crags and flung them into the water; of the island of Olkhon in the north; and of Baikal's only daughter, the beautiful Angara and how, when she ran away to her lover, Yenissei, Baikal out of spite threw a crag after her and this same crag still juts out of the water where Angara now begins.

As I listened I was filled with a sinister feeling. It seemed to me that I already knew what he was telling me, or had known it at one time and forgotten it, but I felt that nothing was quite as he told it; the names of people and places were similar but not those I had once heard. I was unable to recall exactly what they were but I kept wanting to contradict what he said . . .

Then Vitya sang a song:

In ancient times, so long ago,
the earth shook with a mighty quake.
And the Blue Mountain was all engulfed
by the now still waters of the Baikal lake.
The lake and her shores are strewn
with boulders from that mountain.
All else was swept far and away
on the back of the lake's swift rivers.
The fishermen all still love to tell
this wondrous, magical legend.
Their children's children
know it as the living truth.
The only riddle yet unsolved is
who was the first to tell the tale . . .

By this time the waves had begun to splash down on the
rocks behind which we were sitting and the noise of the
swell forced us to talk louder and louder. The far shore
came into view and for the first time I saw the mountains,
which according to Vitya were higher than ours and had
snowy caps on their pointed peaks. It was about forty
kilometres to the opposite shore, though it seemed far more.
Visibility increased to left and right and on each side the
water went up to meet the sky, or the sky came down to
meet the water, and the rather faded, indistinct line of the
horizon could just be made out.

The waves were not just rolling along; it was as if a huge
hand were slapping them, urging them to hurry up. This
seemed to enrage the waves and they vented their anger on
the rocks or on each other, colliding on the rocky shore.
The water started to boil and foam as it spun into whirlpools. There was hardly any wind on the shore; it started

somewhere in the middle of the lake, stirring up waves and chasing them into the shore.

The fishermen took up their positions once again on the sleepers. The waves whipped up on to the sleepers over and over again, thrashing the boys' legs above the knees so that their boots no longer protected them. Despite their wait and Vitya's assurances, there were no more catches, and after a brief half hour, the discouraged fishermen returned to shore. They tipped the water out of their boots, wrung out their trousers and hid their fishing rods for the next time. After we had poured water over the fire, we returned to the embankment and made our way home.

'All we know about fish,' reasoned Vitya, 'is that they are there to be eaten. But we don't know what they get up to, or what goes on in their minds. According to all the laws, they ought to bite when there is a swell and yet, just then, they didn't, which means there must be some explanation which we don't know about. Perhaps we ought to have gone on for a bit longer . . . But I suppose we must content ourselves with what we've got.' And with that, he threw the bag of fish up into the air and it fell with a thud into his arms.

I kept stumbling against the embankment as I walked, for instead of watching where I was going, I contemplated the crags or Lake Baikal. The lake was now dark grey, the sky murky, and the crags, which had been yellow or brown in the sun, had assumed a grey colour too. Although I knew it was the sun which produced the colours, it still seemed that the real reason for everything was, in fact, Lake Baikal; it was not Baikal which looked up at the crags and the sun, but the crags and the sun which looked down on Baikal. That way, they could see themselves, and if the water was calm, then they and everything around would smarten up after looking in the mirror. But if there were waves, then everything shook and became crooked, as it would in a crooked mirror. This would put them all in a bad mood. The sign of bad humour in nature is surely the colour grey, from which the human soul, too, becomes grey.

My own mood at that moment was fair, save for the feeling that I was constantly doing something wrong, or that I had forgotten I don't know what . . . For that reason I was silent, and my new friends probably thought me very unsociable.

The names that I had heard kept going round in my head: Barguzin, Olkhon, Sarma, Angara, and somehow I wanted to modify them, to pronounce them differently perhaps, so as to remember or recognise something . . .

They gave me two of the fish, the biggest, in fact, though I tried to refuse. Since they were not of my own catching, I handed them to my mother and mumbled, 'Here . . . they gave them to me . . . ' Mother was very pleased and said she had always wanted fresh fish.

Going out on to the porch, I looked over into the drop and at once remembered Dead Man's Crag and what had happened the day before. Supper was waiting for me, but I jumped off the steps and ran to the drop. As I ran I was amazed that I could have forgotten about the crag. Perhaps none of it had happened and I had dreamed it in the night. I even stopped when I thought of that. But no – I had left Svetka and run home. Twice I had shut my eyes and had seen the same thing both times. I started running again, then walked fast, then ran again.

I stood at the same place where Svetka had left me to get the cows the day before; I looked for a long time at the crag and the pine and felt very puzzled. It was the same crag, and on its peak the same pine with its four branches. What a wind there was, and how the pine stood up to it! The crag was grey against the grey sky, and the pine, too, was quite difficult to make out. But there was nothing strange about it. I closed my eyes three, four, five times, but saw nothing resembling what I thought I had seen the previous day. The sky was overcast and when I shut my eyes, the silhouette of the pine and crag did not remain behind my closed eyes. All in all, the whole thing seemed quite stupid, ridiculous even.

After supper I ran about the village with the other boys until evening. We climbed a nearby crag and built a dam across the stream. Then a little rain fell and by the time it cleared it was already getting dark. And so ended the second day of my life on the shores of Lake Baikal . . .

2

THE NEXT MORNING, Baikal was light blue, and the sky, naturally enough, was the same colour. The crags round about were golden-brown where there were no trees, and vivid green where trees were growing.

The water no longer looked like glass. I had the feeling that an immense blue tablecloth had been stretched out between the four points of the compass and that bears were walking underneath it, unable to reach the shore. The smooth shining waves were not lapping against the bank but flowing on to it in a film of transparent sky blue.

I followed the shore in the direction of the station, where I had not been before. A boat was moored by the lake and I remembered that on the night we arrived a man had promised me a boat trip. I hoped I would meet him. But there was nobody there. The boat was pulled halfway on to the bank and fixed by a chain to a piece of railway track stuck in the ground. I got into the boat, sat down on the seat and pictured myself floating and rocking on the waves, manipulating imaginary oars.

An aggressive voice interrupted my game: 'Hey, you there, just you get out of that boat!'

The boy was a little older and stronger than me, in short, the archetypal punchy country lad.

I got out of the boat and stood behind it, looking casual. 'Is it yours?'

'What if it is?' he replied with an air of importance.

I kicked a pebble with my feet, slipped my hands into my

pockets and turned my back.

'Hey!'

I turned round.

'What did you do with the shell?' the boy asked, screwing up his eyes menacingly.

'What?'

'I asked what you did with the shell.'

'What shell?' I asked, intrigued.

The boy drew himself up and explained triumphantly: 'The one you've just hatched out of.'

It was such a lovely day, and I was in such a good mood, that I had not the slightest inclination to fight, much less to be beaten. But how could I endure such an insult? I picked up a stone.

'You won't hit me!' he said, scowling harder than ever.

'Oh yes I will!'

'Oh no you won't!'

'I'll hit you on the forehead,' I threatened, brandishing my arm.

'Go on, just try!'

He took off his brimless cap, hung it on the rail the boat was tied to, and advanced towards me. The rail was fifteen or twenty metres from me. I took aim, threw the stone, and just had time to see it flying past him and the boy charging towards me like a bull calf; a second later he pinned me to the ground on my shoulder blades with the palms of my hands flat on the ground.

'You really fell for that one, didn't you? Now I'm going to twist your ears!'

I was squirming in vain under his iron grip. The humiliation reduced me to tears, which merely increased my frustration.

He pressed his knee against my chest and commanded me in a nasty voice: 'Shout "Mummy, Mummy, I want to get married!" If you don't, I'll pull your guts out.'

That would have been preferable to shouting anything so silly! In total desperation I shut my eyes and shook my head, and at once a burning hot liquid ran on to my face. I opened my eyes and saw two trickles of blood streaming from my adversary's nostrils. I pulled myself free and jumped to my feet; he sat on the ground, pressed a finger to his nose and tipped his head back. The whole of the front of my shirt was covered with blood; I rubbed my face vigorously with my shirt-tail, gloating over the sight of the boy who had almost beaten me.

'Why are you just standing there?' he asked thickly. 'Go and get some water in my cap.'

I pulled the cap off the rail, ran to the lake, waited for a wave and scooped up a little water. How odd! I'd been hit on the nose a hundred times but I had never bled like him. I must have dealt him a tremendous knock with my head.

He took the water from the cap and poured it on his nose. The blood turned his whole neck red. I went back to get more water; this seemed to do him good, because he stopped attending to his nose and simply lay down flat on his back.

'I've got a cracked nose,' he said, to exonerate himself. But the sound of his blocked-up nose annoyed him, so he tried threatening me once more. 'The blood will stop in a minute, and then I really will twist your ears.'

'Then I'll hit you on the nose again.'

'No, you won't!'

'I'll make sure I do!'

He raised his nose and pulled a face. 'Last spring I got hit by an oar and it broke my nose. Now whenever you touch it, it starts to bleed. Don't get any ideas though. I'm the strongest around here. Just feel my muscles.'

There was no denying it, he certainly had biceps. But I was terribly pleased with myself, and had already forgotten how I had fallen into his trap. After all, anyone else would have done the same.

Together we washed ourselves and scrubbed the stains. There was no question of going home soaked in blood. We introduced ourselves. His name was Genka. He suggested we should go for a boat trip. We untied the chain and lay down on our stomachs in the bows. The boat did not move.

'What are you doing?' Genka asked, surprised.

I shrugged.

'We've got to raise the bows, and you're pushing them into the ground.'

Immediately the boat began to drift off. I sat in the stern, Genka began to row and we pulled away from the shore.

Genka showed me the bottom of the lake. There was only the gentlest trace of waves, and the further we moved from the bank, the less we felt them. At that depth, the water sparkled incredibly. The rocks underwater were the same as the ones on shore, but much more beautiful. They went down in terraces into the chasm, where they were lost to view. Genka was steering the boat along the edge of it, and on one side we could see the underwater rocks right down to the tiniest pebble; on the other side, the water was inky blue, almost black. Along the rocks under the boat swam shoals of little fish which sometimes fled sideways, and then a big fish would appear, looking like a log. He would move his tail and fins, not seeming to be in a hurry at all.

Everyone knows you can look through a window and see everything that is happening outside, but also you can sometimes see only the windowpane and the specks on it.

The first time I looked into the water, I saw the submerged rocks; the second time, I saw the rocks at the shoreline reflected in it. They were swaying, and seemed to be drawn in green against a backcloth of navy blue; once I had made out the individual trees, I turned towards the shore and looked for the same ones reflected in the water.

Suddenly I noticed the pine on Dead Man's Crag. It was smaller than the palm of my hand, the size of my little finger, but the four branches were clearly visible: two pointing upwards, two down. I looked at the gorge without seeing Dead Man's Crag, which was hidden by the slopes. Not believing my eyes, I looked at the water again: the pine tree was swaying and jerking in front of the bows of the boat. I could have reached out and touched it.

To turn the boat round, Genka thumped the oar on the water and the image disappeared. Then the boat started to rock peacefully on the waves again, but I could no longer see the pine tree. It had disappeared, because the rock at the very bottom of the gorge could not be reflected in the water.

I examined the rocks on the shore: perhaps there was another that looked like Dead Man's Crag? But I looked in vain, I couldn't see anything like it.

That was the moment when I realised that on the first evening I had not been the victim of an optical illusion. What in fact I had seen, instead of the silhouette of the pine with its four branches, was four arms: two raised, reaching towards the sky, and the other two pitifully lowered. I really should not delude myself, I should check and clarify everything. Failure to do so amounted to a cowardly fear of something I did not understand. No more, no less!

Why was I wasting my time?

I told Genka some fib and asked him to put me ashore; soon afterwards I walked through the village in the direction of the gorge, not too fast, not too slow, rather like walking in a dream, but at the same time fully conscious of my actions and gestures, trying hard not to think about the main point of the exercise. As I went along, I whistled to Svetka wading in the water, and called to Yurka who was busy in the vegetable garden near his house; I waved to two other people and managed not to walk any faster as I left the village, although my agitation became greater and greater as I drew nearer to Dead Man's Crag. There it was, very close now, the pine tree completely visible against the backcloth of blue sky; it was even possible to make out the needles on its branches. This time I decided to go as close to the rock as I could, and flatten myself against it to establish beyond any shadow of doubt exactly what was going on.

The path had forked and disappeared to my right and left, and I was facing the scree. I did not stop. Jumping where I could from one stone to another, I circled the very large ones and crawled up the others. Between the stones there were rifts, caves almost, in places. Some stones were really huge rocks; I would climb up one side of them and back down the other. When I decided to rest, and looked up, I realised I had been over zealous. I was right at the very foot of Dead Man's Crag and its lower ledges were hiding the summit and the pine tree. I would have to turn back. But for some reason – I know not what – the first step I took was forwards, not back, and led directly towards the top.

*

Contrary to my wishes and intentions, driven on by some sort of benign doggedness, I began to scale the crag without much hope of reaching the summit, having seen what it was like. But each time I was almost ready to stop, I would say to myself: 'Come on, a little bit further, a little bit further, whatever happens you won't get right to the top.' Strange to say, although each step seemed the last one possible and the next totally inaccessible, my foot always found a foothold, my hand always found a ledge, and I would take the next step like an automaton, against my will, as if the very possibility of hauling myself up were compelling my feet to follow. Sometimes, flattened against the rock, I felt I would not be able to go any higher and would have to go back down, but an external will would drive me conscientiously to look for solutions, to examine the rock to right and left, carefully and minutely, and either I would find a way through to the right, or else I would manage to work my way round the rock to the left, or again I would discover in front of me the gap I needed.

I climbed and climbed and began to worry seriously about how to get back, for I knew the descent would be more difficult. Moreover I was constantly tempted to look down, but was sensible enough not to yield to the temptation.

How much time had passed? How high had I climbed? How much further was it to the summit? I did not ask myself any of these questions. But each time a new wall of rock rose in front of me, I would explore it with my hands and eyes, like a seasoned climber, and would practically die of shock when I realised it was absolutely impossible to climb any higher. My shock soon turned to stupefaction, and the expression on my face at that moment must have been like a sheep's. To stop climbing struck me as an absurdity, a humiliation, a betrayal, which I had not in the least deserved. I recovered my spirits somewhat and saw that I was on a rocky ledge where I could sit down for a rest, and think at last about all that was happening to me. Only when I sat down did I dare turn and look towards the abyss. I was afraid of vertigo, of emptiness and steep slopes, but I felt nothing of that kind. On the contrary, a sensation of total wonder took my breath away.

Before me and below me stretched the realm of azure water and golden-brown rocks. It was not merely that I could see beautiful landscape on the horizon; stretched before me was a world of beauty which words are inadequate to describe, a beauty which was bound to intoxicate you and make you lose your head.

To experience the beauty of the world means to love. It means transforming in one moment all other emotions into love which becomes the unique language in the communication of the soul with the beauty of the world.

This experience of love, this thirst for love, had taken possession of me, and I felt that it was not only lifting me above the world but that it was also making me its equal; I could satisfy my unconscious desire to embrace this marvellous world and laugh with tears of joy at the sight of it.

Subsequently I was to experience the same emotion several times, but each time there was some indefinable element missing, and I could weep with regret that, on that day and at that moment, I had not tried to fly. I still retain the naive conviction that I could have flown that day, could have flown up and over the world, because that was a moment when there was nothing in me to impede it.

Doesn't flying mean crossing the frontier that separates

man from God, unifying one's soul with the soul of the world? Isn't the craving to fly an aspiration towards perfection and purity? The man who eventually succeeded in flying would probably never be able to come back to earth and continue to live the existence of a worm. Perhaps he would die of melancholy, or perhaps indeed he would change the world.

I remember clearly that as I stood on the rocky ledge dominating the gorge I did not live an instant of my own life but an instant of that eternity which, immeasurable as the moment, therefore becomes its true equal.

Then, I remember, all my emotions began to dull, and the weariness of satisfaction set in. I sat down again and the world around me seemed to fragment, to split up into separate objects, to grow heavy and tarnished. The altitude became simply the altitude of the crag, an estimated figure in tens of metres; the height of the sun showed the time; and the coolness of the air heralded the approach of evening.

I tried to return to that sense of elation and purity, but had exhausted my resources. Without my feeling too disillusioned, reality sadly entered my soul, or rather returned to it, and dictated the actions I should take. Along with the sense of reality, I regained my fear of steep slopes and heights, a lack of confidence in my legs, and even a certain regret for having acted rashly.

I got down easily from the ledge. But further on, fear darkened my vision. Suddenly I caught sight of a pass to the right which I had noticed on my way up and which would probably have enabled me to have avoided the shelf altogether and to have climbed above it straight away. And so, because I was terrified of the climb down that awaited me, I began in defiance of all logic to climb up the crag again, avoiding the shelf where I had spent those minutes of such happiness. Or perhaps it was hours?

I surely had to be near the summit, but I could not see it, nor could I see the pine tree.

After another supreme effort I reached a new ledge, much bigger than the first, probably formed by falling fragments of rock. Further on the wall of rock began again, but my ascent had cost me so much strength that deep down I wanted this wall to be unclimbable.

On all fours I crawled along the shelf and when I stood up and took a few steps forward between giant stones, there at the bottom in a niche hollowed out of the rock, sitting on a throne of stone, was . . . an old woman!

This is the point where the most difficult moment of my tale begins.

I have already stated that a miracle is something which takes place despite and contrary to everything. Counter to what exactly? To our experience, of course. Consequently, the more experienced a person is, the more inaccessible a miracle is to him, and the more difficulty he has in accepting one and adapting to it.

The spirit of a child is less firmly tied to the deductions of human experience, although it is already sufficiently weighed down by them. All the emotions of a child still preserve a certain independence – with regard to experience at least – and that is why a child is much more able to trust his emotions than an adult or, as we often say, a wise or sober man.

I often think that people who have apparently taken leave of their senses are no doubt the very people who, in adulthood, have encountered a miracle, clashed with it, but have not been able to dominate it; people who have been unable to reconcile emotions and reason in their souls and have preserved the memory of the miracle in the form of delirium or obsession, because, truly, if a person has held the determinism of the material world to be the inescapable law of existence, can he then go on living when he has clashed with a miracle? Of course not! For him the miracle will become an incurable psychological trauma.

Similarly, I assume that mad people, if they were to recover their sanity, would be able to disclose a multitude of surprising and miraculous things.

When I first saw the old woman, on the rock which nobody had ever climbed before, and which I had had enormous difficulty in reaching, I was initially also in a state bordering on insanity. I could see that old woman so perfectly well, so plainly and clearly, that my amazement was merely surprise pushed to its absolute limit.

If I had encountered an ordinary old woman, I would probably have asked her how she had got there, which would have been an entirely logical question. But in the present circumstances, such a question would have been superfluous. For in no way could she possibly have come to be there as ordinary people come to be in other places.

The woman was so old that it was impossible to imagine any person being older. The lines on her face ran vertically and horizontally, intersecting each other and forming little squares in which other smaller lines crossed over, so that her whole face seemed to consist of nothing but wrinkles. Her hermetically sealed lips were supported by a large, jutting chin which came up to meet her nose, and her eyes were so deeply sunk into the network of wrinkles that the old woman seemed to be blind. She was wearing flowing sky-blue clothes, and this flowing blue enveloped her from head to foot; only her hands, encased in sky-blue gloves reaching to the elbow, contradicted the impression that the blue cocoon contained only a head.

At first glance I could not catch the slightest movement in the old woman's face, and a salutary thought crossed my mind which, if confirmed, could simplify the situation to the point of normality. It occurred to me that perhaps the old woman was a sculpture carved out of some substance or other. This alternative would almost have been a miracle in itself.

But alas! the lines above the eyes began to tremble, and the eyes, small as they were, narrowed even further. There was no possible doubt: the old woman was alive; worse still, she was evil, and the indubitability of this truth filtered through to me, causing a sort of panic. And when I heard her voice, I began to shake with horror.

'Well, come here, you puny little runt!' she said in a rasping, threatening voice; I had never heard such a terrible, hateful voice before.

Frightened to death, I recoiled to the edge of the shelf; when I reached it a stone began to slip from under my foot and fell into the depths with a crash. I took an involuntary step forward, and a second stone slipped from under my foot and thundered into the chasm. I walked towards the old woman; stones slid from under my feet and the din of a landslide rose below the ledge amid a cloud of greyish-yellow dust.

'Stop!' she yelped.

I stood only a metre and a half away from her, and she looked even more hideous when seen from close up.

'Hasn't anyone told you then, you little fox's runt, that climbing up here is forbidden?' she hissed.

'Yes, they did tell me . . . ' I murmured without recognising my own voice.

'So you think you're craftier than the others, you miserable little fool?'

I trembled and said nothing.

'Answer me, why did you climb up here? What did you smell? What did you see? Answer me, little quivering bird, or else I'll send you tumbling down the crag head first.'

Swallowing back my tears, I stammered: 'There's a pine tree up there . . . a pine . . . I didn't want . . . I wanted . . . '

'You're lying, you nasty, cowardly little liar!'

She slapped a blue-gloved hand against her knee and all the blue robes she was wearing seemed to take flight and palpitate as though alive; her face jutted out and looked even more hideous, as always happens when ugliness emerges from something beautiful.

'You're lying!' she yelped. 'There's no pine tree here. There's nothing here. Trees don't grow here!'

'The pine tree is up there!' I resumed in a little more confident a tone, but clinging to my truth as though to a straw.

'There's no pine tree up there!' she rasped obstinately, flushed with anger.

Little by little I was recovering my spirits. If the old woman was unaware that the pine tree existed, then that meant her powers were limited.

'Yes,' I persevered, 'and it's got four . . . arms . . . '

I don't know why I said that. Was it a slip of the tongue? The old woman pounced on it immediately:

'What are you rambling on about, featherless magpie?'

46

'And why are you telling me off?' I was bold enough to ask.

The old woman was dumbfounded, her chin sagged and her eyes grew round.

'Do you know who I am, cuckoo's runt?'

Once again fear reduced me to the state of a blade of grass.

'I am Sarma,' she said, in a majestic, haughty tone.

I knew the name, but was unable to remember where I had heard it.

'I am Sarma!' she repeated, hissing the name. 'I am the great-granddaughter of the Great Sibir. I am omnipotent!'

She suddenly became pensive, and sat completely still in her blue cocoon, gazing through me, or perhaps past me. She was silent for a long while, and again I calmed down a little.

Then, coming back to life, she looked at me suspiciously: 'Are there lots of people down there again?' she asked, as though she wanted to drag a secret out of me.

'Where?'

'The place you came from.'

'I come from Marituy . . . ' I began, but she rushed at me, stretching her outspread fingers towards me.

'Be quiet, be quiet! Prattling little goat! Answer me if you value your life, how do you know that name? That's my son's name!'

'What name?' I asked, not understanding. 'That's what the village is called, on the shores of Baikal.'

'On the shores of what?' she asked again, literally blinded by surprise and fright.

'Maybe,' I said to myself, 'maybe she's just saying she's omnipotent, when really she doesn't know anything.'

'Down below there,' I explained cautiously, 'there's a lake called Lake Baikal and the village on its bank is called Marituy.'

The old woman was thunderstruck.

'How is it that people know those names?' she whispered. 'Could I have whispered them too often, and then the wind spread them over the earth?'

Her head drooped and her expression became pathetic and wretched. I still had not forgotten how those stones had slipped from under my feet and fallen into the abyss, and within me there was a well-matched battle in progress between fear and curiosity. I strove to remember where I had heard the old woman's name – it was not long ago, though then it had sounded different somehow.

Sarma raised her head. 'Go over there,' she ordered.

In the place she was showing me, in front of the wall of rock, there was an enormous boulder, the size of half a room. Whatever had she in mind? Once again, fear drove out all my other feelings.

'What did I tell you!' she said in her hissing voice. 'Go to the rock!'

'But what for?' I yelped.

All the blue material on her body quivered, and I guessed that she was stamping her foot.

'Let me go away. I'll never come here again!'

All her wrinkles shifted malevolently.

'How old are you, little leveret?'

'Twelve,' I replied tearfully.

'Twelve!' she repeated, genuinely astonished. 'Why, don't your parents feed you, or were you born in a year with a bad harvest?'

'Let me go away,' I repeated plaintively.

She screwed up her eyes haughtily, which rendered her even more odious and frightening.

'At twelve my son Marit was already a man. The moon would have fallen into the valley before anyone saw him cry. But as for you, pooh!'

She spat at my feet and pointed towards the big boulder: 'Go where you're told, otherwise your parents will be relieved of the trouble their puny son causes them. Go on!'

I went up to the rock and turned back towards the old woman.

'Push it aside,' she commanded.

I was suddenly struck dumb. Ten strong men could not have managed to make it move.

'Go on!' she shrieked. 'Don't drive me to the limit.'

At the sound of her shouting, my whole body was convulsed, and I leaned against the rock, not even pushing it – what was the use – but even that feeble pressure was enough to make it move. I was not even surprised; rather, I felt a vivid joy in knowing that I could carry out the old woman's order. If only she would stop shouting! I pushed the rock a little harder and it immediately moved half a metre. I lay on it and it moved away to one side, disclosing the entrance to a dark cave.

Sarma took a long look into the blackness of the cave and smacked her lips. 'Go in,' she said, and although her voice was not loud, this was an order.

Now I understood. She was going to hide me in the cave and let me die of hunger in the darkness. With a frantic cry, I rushed away from the cave, leapt past the old woman in one bound and reached the point I had started from; I dangled my legs in order to leap on to a rock lower down, when suddenly it all started again: the stone rolled lazily over on its side and fell into the abyss with the noise of a thunderclap. Next, the rock I had wedged my hand against began to wobble and I was forced to move away from the edge of the abyss and soon found myself once again in front of Sarma's throne of rock.

If it were possible to strike fire out of contempt, I would surely have been burnt to a cinder.

'A coward like you has no right to live. I'd be doing people a favour in getting rid of you . . . I can imagine the shame your mother suffers on your account.' With a grimace of revulsion, she turned away from me and went on talking without turning round or looking in my direction. 'Alas for the people who bring children like you into the world!'

She was silent for a few moments, her lips set. 'Well, seeing you've come here without any invitation, you'll do as I tell you. You will go down at once to see what's happening in there, and then you'll come back and tell me what you've seen. Is that understood?'

What else could I do?

'You'll let me go home, won't you? You'll let me, afterwards?'

I tried to intercept her glance to see if she was intending to cheat me. But the old woman did not turn round. She was looking into the darkness of the cave. 'I'm weary of you, weary,' she hissed. 'If you don't want to be crushed to death by a stone, or turned to stone yourself, you'll do as I tell you!'

From the tone of her voice I realised she must really need me to go. To go and come back . . . Well, we would see what was to happen.

I went towards the cave, and although my heart contracted with fear at every step, I did not stop at the threshold but immediately took a step into the dark.

While I was walking about twenty or thirty paces into the cave, I reviewed in the minutest detail the three days I had spent in the village. And I understood with perfect clarity that what was happening to me at that moment had not occurred suddenly: I had seen, without any warning, an old woman sitting on a throne of rock, and so on. No! It had all started that night when, through the open door of the railway carriage, I had heard an unknown and incomprehensible noise, and even if it had been the sound of the surf, from that moment the whole of my life had travelled alongside a miracle, tightly clasped to it. A miracle indeed exists only for a single moment in defiance of the normal rules. I had seen the old woman on the rock: that was in defiance of the usual rules. And the sequence of events: the stones tumbling down from under my feet, the cave opening up, and everything that was to happen afterwards, all this was governed by rules, different from ours certainly, but rules nevertheless. This was simply a different world, and it was only the moment of initial contact with it which could inspire fear. It should perhaps be said in passing that, if I claimed to have been thinking exactly these thoughts at the time, I should definitely be lying. I was aware, however, of feeling something of the kind.

I had hardly had time to notice the darkness of the cave, when it began to lighten: the light was coming from the place where I was to go down. In front of me were some steps leading down, and then I found myself in a room, or a hall, difficult to define. This round room had a round marble table where big thick books were heaped up, and, starting from the table and diverging on all sides, eleven long tubes were resting with their mouths on eleven niches which were eleven windows, blocked on the outside by the crag. The windows seemed like dead people or blind people, and only the twelfth, through which I had come, gaped open on to the darkness. I guessed that this was the top of a tower and that the tubes were telescopes with which the occupants used to examine the sky long ago, but rocks had grown around the hall, if such a thing were possible. Nobody had been there for an eternity because the ground under my feet, the tubes, the books, everything, was covered with a thick layer of dust on which I walked as though on a carpet; my feet raised the dust which shone like tiny crystals in the atmospheric light of the room, a light which was coming from nowhere and was rendered unusual by its faint blue tinge.

I went up to the table, cautiously dusted one of the books, which, though it made me sneeze, I tried none the less to open. It turned to dust in my hands, and I screwed up my eyes in fright as I thought of the number of years that had passed since the day the occupants had deserted the tower.

I moved away from the table and noticed a flight of stairs leading downwards. I felt the first step with my foot to make sure it really was made of stone, and with infinite care I began to go down.

Wonder gripped my heart when I came down the final step into the room below. This room, or rather hall, was twice as big as the one above; it was round too, and weapons were hanging all over the circular wall: daggers with carved handles and sparkling blades, large and middle-sized scimitars, lances, crossbows, longbows; no two pieces were the same. The floor was carpeted with bear-skins, and every one of them was bigger than the one I had seen at Svetka's house.

Almost at once I noticed a new staircase leading downwards out of the room, but I could not help touching these marvellous things. Here in the hall of weapons there was no dust and each weapon seemed to have been furbished and hung up only a few moments before. I could not work out what metal any particular weapon was made of, but there was no doubt that many of them were silver.

I must have stayed in that room for a long time and was rather scared when I remembered that there were more stairs leading downwards; Sarma had surely not asked me to go just to see the weapons, and I realised I had to find everything there was to see as quickly as possible.

As I set my foot on the staircase, I looked round the hall once again and comforted myself with the thought of seeing all the weapons again on the way back.

This flight of stairs was longer and led me into an immense hall with pillars arranged in two rows forming a sort of corridor, at the end of which I saw something, statues perhaps, where it seemed brighter. The sides of the colonnade on the other hand stood in almost total darkness; here, as upstairs, I could not understand where this strange blue-tinged light was coming from. I followed the corridor in the direction of the statues and had not gone twenty metres when I stopped dead, stupefied and on my guard.

On a high-backed throne set on a small rocky platform sat an old man. At least he seemed to me to be very old under the thick white beard which fell to his chest. His clothes, halfway between a smock and a cloak, were navy blue, and against this background the white beard looked like sea foam . . . White eyebrows covered his eyes. The face looked sad and austere.

At his left hand, her head leaning on the armrest of the throne, sat a little girl of eleven or twelve. Her dark chestnut hair was hanging down from the armrest and the old man's hand was resting on the child's knees. The armchair she was sitting on was somewhat smaller than the throne, but its back was just as high. On the little girl's left, with his head resting on outstretched paws, lay a small black dog with a brown patch above his eyes.

And all three of them . . . were asleep.

From twenty paces away I could not detect the slightest movement, and yet I was absolutely certain they were not statues. I even seemed to hear them breathing, although in fact I could hear nothing. I knew. I was looking at living people and was no longer as amazed as when I had first seen Sarma. I knew now that it was to them that the old woman had sent me.

I approached them very quietly and when there were only three or four metres between me and the platform, the little dog raised his head and looked at me in astonishment. The curls quivered against the old man's arm, and the little girl opened her eyes with a great effort as though waking from a long and painful sleep, and she too raised her head and looked at me as if she could not believe her eyes.

Her eyes were the same shade of deep blue as the old man's robes, and despite their expression of great surprise, they were so sad that everything in the room was immediately filled with sadness. The sadness pierced my heart too and it began to hurt, and I felt worse than I had ever felt in my life before.

The little girl was so pretty that I could not depict her

beauty in words, and I felt I could have lived to my dying day without needing anything other than to gaze at her incessantly.

Her eyelashes fluttered and she said, in a voice that evoked the murmur of a stream flowing over stones: 'Look, Father.'

I understood what she said but she seemed to pronounce the words differently from us, in a quite exceptional way; none of the sounds was indistinct, but it seemed to me that she was speaking only in vowels.

Her father (I could see now that he was not as old as he had appeared at first on account of his beard and white hair) opened his eyes slowly, with difficulty – eyes the same colour as the child's, but even sadder – no, they did not exactly express sadness, rather pain, and possibly even something else besides.

All three looked at me for a long while in silence as if, during that time, they were recalling all that had happened to them before I came, and right from the start, although their gaze was fixed on me, they were really looking inwards at themselves; when I felt they were at last seeing me properly, the old man's lips trembled (in my mind I called him 'the old man') and I heard his soft voice, muted and very sad: 'How did you get here?'

'Sarma sent me,' I replied in a trembling voice.

'Sarma!' echoed the little girl, and she pressed against her father's hand, looking at me with the same sadness.

'Sarma!' repeated the old man tonelessly.

I could not for the life of me gain any clue from his intonation which would have helped even a little to shed light on this whole strange, incomprehensible and painful adventure.

'Is she still up here?' asked the little girl, and again her voice told me nothing.

'Yes.'

'And you . . . Where do you come from? And why has she sent you here?' asked the old man, not showing any particular interest.

'She told me to come and see, and to tell her all about it . . . I come from Marituy.'

Both of them were startled by the name, especially the little girl. Without waiting for a reply I hastened to explain: 'Out there, down below, there's a lake called Baikal . . . '

The old man's eyebrows jerked with surprise and the little girl stared at him in stupefaction.

'On the shore,' I went on, 'there's a village. Its name is Marituy.'

Again their gaze, although fixed on me, seemed to drift away; again they began to think about something or remember something which lent their faces a deeper expression of sorrow.

'There's water all over the place out there, Father,' explained the little girl in a voice full of grief.

'But people are living there again,' replied her father, an anxious hope seeming to enter his voice.

'How is it that they know the names?' murmured the little girl.

I grew bolder and went up to the platform where the thrones stood.

'Why . . . are you . . . here?' I asked timidly.

The little girl closed her eyes and laid her head on her father's hand again. With the other hand he stroked her hair, and when he looked at his daughter there was so much grief in his eyes that they turned a darker colour.

'I'm weary, Father,' the child whispered.

'She's weary,' he told me, 'you must go now.'

The little dog laid his head on his paws and closed his eyes.

'Perhaps, if Sarma allows me, I can come back tomorrow?' I asked, fearful of meeting with a refusal. But I heard nothing. The old man's hand froze on the child's head and he too closed his eyes wearily. As if he had not been speaking to me a moment before, as if the hall had not echoed to the sound of that voice which pronounced words so strangely. But only 'as if' . . . The little girl's voice was echoing in my heart and seemed to pierce it with thousands of needles of compassion.

At first I walked backwards, unable to turn my back on the two recluses, but finally I had to make up my mind to do so; as I started back up the stairs I kept turning round several times, hoping to catch the slightest movement in their frozen posture, ready to rush towards them, to say or do something.

Sarma! It was Sarma who had to tell me why they were there, who they were, what she was doing on the crag; these questions, and others, made me climb the stairs of the ghostly castle without sparing a passing glance at all that was in the upper rooms.

The daylight blinded me as I emerged from the cave and I stood blinking for a while before running towards Sarma.

Her face was triumphant and sarcastic. She didn't have to explain anything to me: I knew that she was responsible for the sadness I had seen in the little girl's face. The whole thing was Sarma's fault . . .

'So what, then?' she asked, screwing up her eyes and sniggering nastily.

'So what?' I asked her in return, not hiding the hatred I felt for her.

'Did they ask anything from me?'

'No.'

A shadow of vexation flickered across the old woman's face, quickly replaced by an incomprehensible delight.

'What about the little girl?'

'She didn't ask anything either.'

'In the Valley of the Young Moon even the little girls were brave and didn't snivel like some people . . . ' she said, obviously for my benefit.

But all of a sudden, the sarcasm and scorn disappeared from her face and it became as sad and pathetic as the faces of the two captives in the cave; she seemed to collapse altogether into her absurd sky-blue robe, her head flopped feebly to one side, and it seemed that tears were about to pour from her eyes at any moment. But I did not see even the tiniest tear. All she did was mumble words I could not catch, and nod her head gently. All my ill feeling towards her vanished. I had an urge to speak kindly and simply to her, and vaguely thought that such an approach could resolve the terrible misunderstanding at the root of the sorrow and grief of those three creatures . . .

'Grandmother!' I said gently in a low voice.

She jumped with surprise, as though coming back to earth.

'Grandmother! Do I look like a grandmother?' she asked, with a weird giggle.

She didn't look like a grandmother, she looked like a great-great-grandmother.

'Very well then, you may really call me Grandmother.'

She giggled again, and became appallingly hideous,

especially when she attempted to roll her eyes, as little girls do when they show off or give free rein to their imagination.

She really isn't normal, I thought.

'Why are they down there . . . and you here . . . and everything?'

Her lips clenched, her chin moved up towards her nose, and her eyes screwed up, sparkling with evil.

'So you want to learn what you don't know, little urchin? Is your chicken's spirit capable of sheltering the knowledge of the spirit of real men? Won't it be torn apart, won't it burst like a bubble? And if that hare's brain of yours is equal to understanding the thoughts of heroes, is it capable of knowing great grief and joy? What do you know about knowledge, pathetic little runt? Knowledge is what summons people to perform great deeds, it's not a pebble you swallow and then rub your stomach afterwards.'

I did not really understand what she was saying. I did, however, have the feeling she was scolding me, but I was no longer afraid of her rebukes.

'No,' I said maliciously, 'if it's a secret, then of course . . . '

'A secret?' she repeated mockingly. 'What do you know about secrets? Seeing you've come here without any invitation, however, I'll tell you something . . . '

She squinted at me and clicked her lips. 'Do you love your parents, little spider with the delicate hands?'

Why was she asking about my parents?

'If you didn't love them, that would be the last straw!' she snorted impatiently. 'Other parents would throw a runt like you over a cliff to escape the shame.'

Why was she vilifying me like this? I was no less sturdy than other lads of my age, and indeed I was more agile than some.

'Listen well!' she said solemnly, raising her blue-gloved finger. 'Listen! You've seen a lot here, you've heard things and you'll hear more. But be warned, rather than tell anyone at all down there, you'd do better to swallow your tongue. Because, before your tongue had stopped turning in your mouth, your parents would be dead. I'm binding your tongue for twenty-five years! Have you understood?'

I froze with horror. I might betray the secret unwittingly, I might lose consciousness and talk. I could picture myself telling the story of Dead Man's Crag and seeing my mother drop dead, and my father after her, without any possibility of calling them back to life.

'Aha!' cawed the old woman sarcastically. 'It seems you're beginning to understand what a secret is. You imagine a secret is a trifle you can play guessing games with? A secret will never belong to you alone. Give away a secret, and you harm somebody else . . . And that has to be paid for. You will live to regret your curiosity.'

Perhaps I was already beginning to regret it? I can't remember.

'You want to know why the old man and his daughter are shut away down there, inside the crag. I'll tell you.'

Her gaze clouded over, her eyes sank deeper and deeper into her head. 'I'll tell you. That little girl, she and her father . . . '

She seemed to falter. 'Do you know who her father is?'

However could I have known?

'He is Baikolla, Prince of the Valley of the Young Moon. There was a time when the whole crescent of the valley was under his rule. And there he sits down below, and there he'll sit for ever because he committed a horrible crime. He and his wretched daughter . . . they killed my younger son . . . '

She whispered the last few words as if she were deepening their meaning and was frightened by it. Then she repeated in a whisper several times, 'Killed! Killed! Killed!'

She had forgotten about me and was looking towards Baikal. 'It was so long ago, yet I feel as if it happened yesterday.'

Then she was silent for a long while. For my part, I began to think; I could not conceive that the little girl and her father could have killed anyone. Maybe it had happened accidentally, but then why keep them for ever inside the crag? No, that wasn't it. I remembered the expression of eternal sorrow in the eyes of the captives, and perhaps they also reflected a certain guilt . . . Prince Baikolla . . . Baikal . . . Was her son called Marit? The village of Marituy . . . How strange and incomprehensible it all was.

The little girl's eyes kept appearing relentlessly before me. I could hear her sad voice, and the opinion took root in my mind that there was an injustice somewhere in all this. It was an injustice that originated in the old woman, even though she claimed the prince had killed her son. No, I was convinced the little girl could not be guilty of anything.

I was going to question the old woman but she forestalled me.

'Are you still here? What more do you want? Get out of my sight!'

Obediently, I nodded my head.

'But remember your parents!'

She needn't have bothered to say that.

'Can I come tomorrow?' I asked timidly.

But the old woman had withdrawn into herself and could no longer hear.

I went down the crag and strangely, though I didn't think about it at the time, not a single stone came away from under my hands or my feet. And it was only when I reached the path near the fork that I looked up at the crag and a shiver ran down my spine: I had the feeling that I had not climbed down from there but had suddenly just found myself at the bottom.

From here the crag really did seem dead, and at its summit the pine tree with the four branches appeared on the whole like any other pine; but now I knew the secret of the crag, and I tried to see again in my mind's eye the castle where Prince Baikolla was imprisoned with his daughter before it blended into the rock.

Night had fallen without my noticing.

'Hey-ho!' called a child's voice behind me.

I turned round, and for some reason did not immediately recognise Svetka. Perhaps it was because the picture of the other little girl, pretty and sorrowful, was somehow imprinted in my eyes.

Svetka's eyes shone brightly, in keeping with her name; she was very cheerful and nimble, like a grasshopper, which made me even more sorry for the girl who remained behind in the blue half-light of the crag.

'Your mother's been looking for you. Where were you? Are you still staring at Dead Man's Crag? It really has scared you stiff!'

Svetka was jumping around me on the stones and giggling inanely. What did she know about that rock? I had only to say one word and instantly, like a stroke of lightning, my father and mother would drop dead. I clenched my teeth so hard that they hurt.

'Let's go and find the cow!'

I made no objection, and we both circled the rock to the left, went a little way up the gorge, found Svetka's cow by the particular note of her bell among the silver birches, and led her out, or rather we followed her as she set off towards the fork with a lively and businesslike step, waving her tail and treading the stones on the path.

Two other cows followed her; Svetka knew who they belonged to and what their names were, whereas I could not have told them apart, even at close range.

At home, predictably, my mother scolded me a little, then gave me some reheated cabbage soup and asked: 'Where have you been?'

I choked on my soup. She could not imagine the risk she was running by asking me that question.

Before going to bed I went out on to the front porch and looked for a good long time in the direction of Dead Man's Crag. It was cool. A breeze was blowing from the gorge and from the direction of Baikal I could hear the same noise as I had heard on the night we arrived. From there too came the peculiar smell which had struck me so forcibly then. I knew now that it was the smell of coolness and Lake Baikal.

'There's water all over the place out there.' I remembered what the young captive of Dead Man's Crag had said. So, at one time there wasn't any. What had there been? Roll on tomorrow morning! I knew that as soon as I got up I would go there at once, I would scale the rocks and ledges again. Sarma had not forbidden me to come, so that meant she would let me.

Now at any rate I knew the secret, though not the whole of it. But one day I would know it all.

I had a premonition that at a certain point I would be something other than the witness of the secret. The four branches of the pine tree that grew on Dead Man's Crag were four arms and, although two of them hung down involuntarily, the other two reached towards the sky, begging for help . . .

That night I dreamed that my father and mother were standing in front of me and I was starting to tell them about Sarma and the castle in Dead Man's Crag; then I saw Mother close her eyes and fall over backwards, while my father, too, closed his eyes and fell forwards at my feet. I screeched wildly and went on screaming, even after I was awake.

My mother shook me by the shoulder and asked in a frightened voice: 'What's the matter, my dear? Calm down!'

I hugged her and kissed her, and she did her best to soothe me, not understanding at all. But all at once I thought of my father and cried out: 'Where's Papa? Is he alive? I want him to come!'

My father too then sat on my bed and I went back to sleep, holding both my parents by the hand.

3

I SLEPT UNTIL ABOUT TEN O'CLOCK and had great difficulty in waking up; one minute I would seem about to wake, the next minute I would go back to sleep and dream that I was getting up, dressing and setting off for somewhere. In fact I was in bed all the time, with the blanket pulled up over my head. At last I woke up properly and spent some time considering the reasons for my bad mood. All at once I remembered everything that had happened without feeling sure that it was not a dream.

Finally I leapt up like a scalded cat and dressed hurriedly, furious with myself for having slept so long. What I saw out of the window explained my bad mood. The world outside seemed to have been transformed. Everywhere from the sky to the ground was covered with a sullen greyness, and the gloom was even seeping in through the window. There was no blue sky or brown rocks or greenery on the slopes: wherever had the colours disappeared to?

It's going to rain, I thought with horror. It was still possible, of course, to climb rocks in the rain, but it amounted to suicide. And the higher you climb on wet rocks, the greater the risk of breaking your neck if you fall.

'Maybe it'll clear up,' I said to myself, slipping on my jacket and going out on to the front steps. But it was hopeless. The strip of sky above the gorge was blotted out by great black clouds. They advanced from Dead Man's Crag, slowly, yet so implacably and so tightly packed that I felt that somewhere beyond the mountains a vast quantity of clouds had piled up, and would, when there was no more room in the sky, start tumbling down, filling the gorge to its rocky rim.

Yurka went leaping past the house, on his way to Baikal; he waved his hand at me and I could not understand whether he was beckoning me or simply being friendly. Then Valerka also went by at a run and he too waved at me, but he turned back and when he reached the corner of the house he called: 'Let's go to Baikal! The raft has come in with the Barguzin!'

Valerka's raised thumb intrigued me, and just as I was, with bare feet inside my boots, I followed him, fully aware that when I got home again there would be worse trouble in store than there had been the day before. My parents were admittedly busy with settling into the house, but they were not likely to go on excusing me indefinitely.

Taking the same path as Valerka, I jumped under the bridge and sped to the shore, gasping at the sight of the waves. Then I jumped for a long time on the stones along the shoreline in the direction of the place where I had been fishing with Yurka two days before.

The raft rose from the water like some great building, almost as big as the ferry-boat, yet so indefinite that when I saw the railway sleepers tossing about on the waves, I would have run on, had Valerka and Yurka not halted.

'Just look at that!' exclaimed Valerka in admiration.

Thinking that he meant the waves, I nodded.

That was what it meant to be getting accustomed to extraordinary things! The waves were spectacular and yet I had run along the shore for two hundred metres at least without staring wide-eyed, without being rooted to the spot. And to think this was the Barguzin! That was the local name for the swell from the north; or, to be more exact, it was the name of the north wind which stirred up the water and drove the waves towards us. The waves thrashed on to the shore as if someone were throwing them up from the deep. They advanced in even ranks, but in the distance this movement became blurred and the lake seemed to be frozen into black lumps which suddenly came to life close to the shore where they unloaded their vexation and weariness. The shore itself, a stretch of pebbly ground below the railway line, seemed to present its shoulders to their malice and fury, and its rigidity increased the irritation of the waves, driving some of them quite mad with rage.

But that was the very last thing I wanted to think about; and once I had understood that much, I was able to see that there really was no hostility between the lake and the shore, and that it had been merely the product of my imagination.

'You just watch how I'm going to crash!' threatened the wave, not very seriously, whipping up foam as it came in.

'Oh, oh, I was so scared!' whispered the shore, pretending to tremble with its stone vertebrae.

Nevertheless, when a pall of grey wrack smothers the sky, when the waves are black or navy blue by turns, and the shore seems to have hidden its head under stone armour to await the onslaught, what follows is neither a conflict nor a game, but work: the tasks of the waves and the shore are different, and should one wave come and strike a rock with a different sound from another, or should it slip its wet tentacles between the rocks, that is simply because it is not wasting its strength, because it has no need to, for that is not its job.

Whatever your dreams or thoughts, it is always wonderful to stand on the rock nearest to the water, to watch the waves just in front of you running in on to your legs, to feel that dangerous giddiness catch at the heart as you see yourself confronting and resisting an element which is not only stronger and greater than you, but also totally different in terms of its nature and destination.

Valerka and Yurka were arguing about something, raising their arms and waving in various directions. Although I was close to them, I could hear only exclamations through the incessant crashing and roaring of the waves. I had by then noticed the sleepers jammed between the stones and hopping sideways as each wave came in. I saw that they were fastened together with metal and I guessed that this must be the raft; I was not really disappointed, more puzzled, and felt unable to see the point of such a precarious contraption which would be terrifying even to set foot in, whereas rafts, after all, were for sailing on.

I jumped on to the big flat rock where Valerka and Yurka were stamping about, and called to them, pointing to the raft: 'Is that it?'

Valerka showed me his thumb again, but I was quite unable to understand his enthusiasm.

'We've got to hide it! We can use it for fishing and diving!'

There were only two boats in the whole village. It was obviously more practical to fish from a boat, and even more so to swim from one, although knowing that the lake was terribly deep in places rather put me off that. I reckoned that the raft consisted of only eight sleepers, and I felt that I'd sooner never swim again than venture one metre from dry land on a raft like that.

'It's small,' I shouted, right into Valerka's ear.

He opened his eyes wide.

'*We* fish from three sleepers.' And he held three fingers under my nose.

We had to hide the raft from the other children – and also from grown-ups. The three of us toiled away for three hours under the waves, soaked to the skin, of course, heaving the raft behind the promontory among the huge rocks where it was invisible from the embankment.

Carrying it meant dragging it along the shore by means of a wire slipped through the clamp, and taking advantage of the flow of the waves to pull it along. When a wave broke on the shore, and thus on the raft, we would throw ourselves underneath it to prevent the raft being pushed back under or between the stones, where it was in danger of getting stuck, in which case we would not have been strong enough to extricate it. We then spent quite a long time tying it to the rocks so that it would not be dislodged by the storm.

As long as we kept moving we did not feel the cold, but as soon as we sat down to rest after our exertions and looked at each other, we began to get worried; not only me but my friends too, the true children of Baikal.

'Let's go home,' said Yurka in a sullen tone of voice. 'We've got to get dry. Luckily my mother's away.'

Valerka's face clouded over, as did mine. Our mothers were at home.

While I was being undressed and dried, I got half a dozen cuffs round the ear, heard countless reproaches and had to make a thousand and one promises regarding my future conduct. I bravely swallowed all the disgusting stuff known as medicine and, in short, showed myself in my most favourable light and freely admitted my imprudence.

Neither this treatment, however, nor the fur coat I was wrapped up in, nor my father's pedagogical encouragements ('nothing's going to happen to him; he's a man, not a girl') could save me from the chill which began that evening with a raised temperature, degenerated into delirium during the night, and into pulmonary congestion the following morning.

On the whole, I pulled through relatively well. At the end of the second week I went out on to the front steps, where I stayed for a while in the warmth of the sun; watching it slipping surreptitiously from one crag to another, before rising up slowly above them, where it hung suspended over the gorge, bringing the side of it to life, and revealing all the splendid colours of the rocks and the trees.

Mother told me that while I was delirious I had been talking about an old woman. My heart turned to ice. But I reasoned with myself that if I had been talking in a delirium then, first, it had not been done consciously and could therefore not be considered a disclosure and, second, nobody would take seriously anything I had said while I was raving, all of which meant I had not betrayed my secret.

All the same, I was scared. This was my own reasoning, and I did not know how Sarma would view it.

I was still very weak and my exhaustion modified my impatience to go back to Dead Man's Crag as soon as possible, to run off to it forth with; from the porch where I sat I could see the crag and make out the pine tree on top of it, although I could not see the branches from so far away.

Valerka paid a flying visit to tell me breathlessly how he and Yurka were sailing on the raft, fishing from sandbanks, and managing brilliantly to hide the raft from the other children.

Genka also stopped in front of the porch to tell me his grandfather had killed a huge wild bear with a single shot;

even though he was seventy, Grandad was still a crack shot, no doubt about it!

After lunch I was put back to bed where I read *The Last of the Mohicans* without much interest; I would constantly catch myself letting my eyes wander over the lines, knowing in advance that Uncas, the son of Chingachgook, was going to get killed on the last page; I could not understand why people had to write stories, the sense of which was lost through death, the more so when it was accidental, as in the case of this novel.

In my own life, for instance, it was not at all like that. Everything that had happened to me from the beginning – I took our move to Baikal as the starting point – was full of meaning; the events which had already taken place, together with those of the present, were like a ball of thread unwinding; the end of the thread was still hidden – though I felt sure it would be connected to what happened inside the crag – and I was convinced that the end would be something important, not just for my own life, but important in a general way for everyone, and for that reason there could not be a bad or sudden ending, though perhaps there would be no ending at all, just as a life which has newly begun seems to have no ending.

Sarma had been right to warn me that knowledge could be harmful, but that was unimportant: it is always more interesting to know than not to know. Of course it is better to know things one can tell everyone else about. But even when one can't say anything, it's still interesting.

Several times I would get up, thinking I was fit enough to run to the crag, but each time I had to sit down on a step, racked by dizziness and frustration.

Later, when I was sure of myself and completely recovered,

my parents told me not to leave the porch, and they watched over me so zealously that I had no opportunity of slipping away from them.

It was high summer, the weather was glorious and the children had deserted the village again. It was not yet the season for walnuts and wild berries, but it was ideal weather for swimming. It was only from the stories my friends told me as they rushed by that I knew of their adventures in the lake: who had dived the deepest, who had crossed Marituy Bay on a single sleeper, who had stayed longest under water hugging a huge stone to his chest.

I grew more and more humiliated by my fate, my ridiculous illness, and my parents stubbornly keeping me at home just when the children were having most fun.

The events on Dead Man's Crag also increased my anxiety. Sometimes I was beginning to think nothing had happened, that I hadn't climbed the crag, but had dreamed it all when I was delirious; the sun which shone on me and on the world was so bright, the smell of greenery from the slopes of the gorge so delightful, and in general the real world so beautiful and open to the senses, that it was impossible to believe a place devoid of joyous sunshine could exist anywhere.

Finally the day came when my mother forbade me on pain of a whipping to go anywhere near the shores of the Baikal. That meant I was free! The first thing I did, of course, was to run to the lake.

The children's beach was below the railway embankment at a slight distance from the bridge, on a narrow strip of the shore near the old pier. There would be several camp fires burning even on very hot days because the children used to swim all day long until sunset, and I already knew what the water temperature was like. Despite my initial disobedience, I did not dare to swim. I did not even go right on to the beach but stayed at a distance, staring with narrowed eyes at the glittering surface of the lake which for some reason had a faint tinge of green that day, perhaps because the sides of the gorge and the mountains all along the railway were ablaze with vivid green.

There were no waves, only blue-green circles which spread out from the beach to a not-too-distant point before vanishing into the solemn and dignified stillness of the infinite expanse of water. The lake's serenity made me feel placid and benign so that I refused categorically to think that beneath the delicate, sparkling glass of its surface there could be an abyss several hundred metres deep where eternal darkness and peace prevailed as in a cemetery. I didn't want to think about it, but think about it I did, and I felt quite faint at the thought of drowning in that infinite darkness, at a depth even aqualung divers never reached.

And probably by gloomy association with the unfathomable depths of the water, my thoughts returned to Dead Man's Crag, its captives buried alive, and the unsolved secret demanding to be unravelled.

My journey to the crag on that occasion seemed to me to be three times as long, and the climb ten times harder – probably the result of my great impatience, or perhaps of my weak condition following my illness.

Before the final assault, I stood still, straining my ears. I thought I could hear Sarma mumbling, or the rustling of her blue robe. But it was nothing. I was even beginning to doubt if she was there. Consequently, I almost leapt with fright on to the last ledge. How ghastly that old woman was, sitting on her throne of rock, framed in the aureole of her ethereal blue robe.

'So you have flown here after all, little fledgling!' she said, not without some surprise, though above all with venom, for she seemed incapable of opening her mouth without hatred or nastiness.

I said nothing in reply. I only swallowed, trying to get my breath back.

'Did I give you permission to come back?' She screwed up her eyes, which made her look like Baba Yaga in the fairy-tale. 'Because I let you out alive from here once, you think I'll do the same again . . . Or did you imagine that I was missing you?'

She began to snigger, hunching her shoulders up to the nape of her neck, so that her chin seemed to sink on to her knees.

Who could tell what was going on inside her head? The very thought made me shiver.

'What is it then, have you bitten your tongue with fear?' she asked.

I was quite unable to find an answer. I needed to go down into the crag and I was not prepared to stay chatting to this evil old woman.

'I wanted . . . ' I stammered, 'I thought . . . '

'You thought,' she replied, shaking with laughter and setting up ripples of blue in her garment. 'Can you think? It doesn't seem like it. Is it possible that you have the necessary material for thinking inside your chicken's head?'

This was too much. I scowled evilly and began to snarl.

'Oh, I'm so scared!' she cried, feigning fear. 'Why have you stayed away thinking for so long that I've even had time to forget you?'

'I've been ill.'

'Ill!' she exclaimed. 'No doubt fear gave you hiccups and you've been made to drink milk.'

'It's not you I've come to see!' I blurted out. What was the use of talking to her, far less trying to explain!

The old woman drew herself up arrogantly.

'A visit from you is the last thing I need! Last time your croaking and yapping gave me a headache for three moons!'

She had taken offence after all.

'All right then,' she muttered. 'Go where you want. But the day will come when you'll regret ever having known the path that leads here.'

'Caw! Caw!' I murmured, and headed for the stone.

I leant on it in some dread. It was so huge that I did not believe I would manage to push it aside a second time. But it moved as before and, without stopping, I ran through the cave, the hall with the telescopes and the armoury, contenting myself with running a hand over one of the tubes and glancing at the sparkling swords and daggers. By contrast, when I reached the final step into the hall with the pillars, I entered very softly and froze as I contemplated the silhouettes of the two figures at the other end. I walked towards them without a sound, without even hearing my own footsteps. But when I came within a few yards of the stone platform, and before I had even come to a halt, the little black dog with the brown circles round his eyes raised his head, just as he had done on the previous occasion. I was not looking at him, however, but at the little girl. During those past days I had somehow forgotten just how beautiful she was, how extraordinary and sad she looked, even in sleep. Once more, pity seared my heart, supplanting all thoughts and desires.

She was still sitting down with her head leaning on her father's hand, and her hair, tied close to her head with a blue ribbon, fell on to the old man's knees; his hand was still resting on his daughter's hair in exactly the same position as the time before, as if so many days had not gone by since then, as if I had only left the room for one minute.

She raised her head and looked at me – albeit fleetingly – as if remembering something, and straight afterwards I saw in her face an expression of joy, momentary but no less real. Without lifting his head, her father looked at me too, as if through his lashes, but his expression was not in the least hostile.

'Did Sarma let you come?' the little girl asked.

'Yes,' I replied rather uncertainly, because for all I knew I might never be allowed back another time.

'Tell her Baikolla thanks her for her kindness.'

There was no irony in his voice. He was thanking her sincerely. But why? It meant, I thought, that he really had killed her son. But the little girl? She couldn't have killed anyone.

'Tell us,' she asked, 'what's happening now in the valley.'

'Valley? What valley?'

'Child, there's no valley down there any more,' replied the father with grief and bitterness.

'Yes . . . ' she agreed sadly. 'There's no valley down there any more. But you . . . Where you live . . . and the others with you . . . tell us!'

'There's a lake, I told you last time, and it's called Lake Baikal.'

'You pronounce that word incorrectly. Why is that?'

I shrugged. 'Everyone calls it that and it's written like that in books and maps.'

'Do the people of your tribe have books and maps?' asked the father, clearly not so much surprised as delighted.

I realised that they had no idea of our way of life and that if I began to describe it I would run out of time; what I wanted was to find out why they were here, and who they were and who Sarma was. I had to know everything.

I asked them a question in return: 'And you . . . Why are you here? And where . . . where was the valley?'

The little girl looked at her father in bewilderment, as if asking his permission to answer. But he remained silent, looking calmly at me, but whether or not he actually saw me, I did not know.

'Did Sarma give you permission to ask that question?' the little girl asked cautiously.

How they dread her, I thought. The old woman had not given me permission to ask, but nor had she forbidden me. I decided to resort to guile. 'She told me to keep silent about anything I find out.'

'Father, may I tell him the legend?' the little girl asked timidly.

'Sarma knows what she's doing, since she's let him come here. Tell him!'

He lowered his head on to his chest and closed his eyes.

'You must sit down. It's forbidden to listen to the legend standing up.'

Her eyes shone and became animated, and she looked lovelier than ever. I could only try to guess what she would be like if she were to smile or laugh, if she were taken out into the sunlight, on to the edge of the lake, if she were covered with flowers . . .

I was about to sit down on the little platform where the

thrones were, but the floor was marble and therefore very cold; remembering the bear-skins, I ran off to the hall above, grabbed the nearest skin from the floor, took it down and spread it out next to the dog at the girl's feet.

The child's eyes were burning. She no longer took any notice of me, but waited impatiently for me to get ready to listen.

'Are you ready?' she asked severely.

I nodded, and sat completely still.

'Long, long ago,' she began, 'when the nights of mankind were so dark and the moon was not yet in the sky, a great tribe of good and valiant men lived on the shores of the distant ocean. The men fished in the ocean, hunted animals in the surrounding taiga, and carved beautiful things from wood and stone which they gave as gifts to one another. The people had everything they needed to make them happy. They did not sing songs about happiness; their songs were happiness itself.

'But one fine day, Black Death came out of the ocean and swooped down on the tribe, sparing neither children nor old people, men nor women.

'Death lay in wait for the people on the shore and in the water; it entered houses, tracked men down on the paths of the taiga, and none could escape it, none could stand up to it, because the healers and the sorcerers were dying like the rest and their wisdom was powerless in the face of that Death which rose from the ocean.

'From morning to night the elders of the tribe deliberated the means of saving their people, though many were struck down while they meditated, and did not live to see another dawn.

'The people stopped working and simply waited to die.

'If they woke in the morning they were merely surprised to be still alive, and when they found none of their nearest and dearest among the living, they no longer grieved.

'In the encampments songs and voices fell silent, and no one left his house; people began to die of hunger because nobody wanted to go on the ocean or into the taiga. Everyone wanted to die in his own house.

'But four brothers, the boldest hunters of the tribe, went to visit the elders. The eldest brother was called Baikolla, the second Barguzzi, the third Olkhonna, and the youngest Burri.

'The four brothers told the elders that, while they had been out hunting, they had strayed far from the shore and discovered a place beyond the taiga where the sun shone in a land of blue mountains; there they had found a herd of deer and wild boar, driven over there by forest fires, and flocks of birds which had taken refuge there till springtime.

'In a place where the beast and bird lived, they said, man could live too. And it might be that Death, begotten of the ocean, would not go further than the ocean.

'The four brothers proposed to lead the tribe to that distant land to which no road led, where no man had been, and from which no one had come.'

The little girl fell silent. She was impassioned, her eyes were full of joy and pride, her voice trembled and her hands gripped the arm of the chair.

'Are you listening?' she asked sternly.

'Yes, yes, do go on.'

'The people had no other hope of survival, and so, having buried their dead, they gathered together their most valued possessions, laid the dying on stretchers, and set off into the depths of the taiga, towards the land where the brave hunter brothers led them.

'Death grew anxious and restless. It refused to let go its grip on the people and threw itself after them into the darkness of the taiga, caught up with them at their overnight camp and struck down the first it found in the shadows.

'The next morning the people buried their dead and set off again. But Death also advanced and soon caught up. In the evening it entered the body of one, in the morning it clutched the garments of another, and at midday it grabbed a third victim by the throat.

'But the people went on and went on; they were already far from the ocean. Death, however, without fear of losing its way back, raged furiously.

'The people had already reached the first mountain range full of gorges and chasms, when Death finally guessed who was leading the people away from it; at night it stole into the heart of one of the brothers, the one named Olkhonna. The next morning a stentorian voice roused the people from sleep.

'Olkhonna, standing on a rock at the edge of an abyss, was calling to them: "Brothers! Death has entered into me! This chasm is deep, make use of the time Death will take to climb back out; and escape as far as you can."

'With these words, Olkhonna threw himself into the chasm and the people leapt to their feet, picked up the sick and the exhausted, carried them on their backs and, without uttering a sound from morning until night, they fled to the place where the three surviving brothers led them.

'At that time the moon was not yet in the sky and the people could travel only by day. Death took a long time to emerge from the chasm but finally it succeeded and threw itself in pursuit of the people, caught up with them, and entered into Burri, the youngest of the brothers.

'The people were surrounded by mountains on all sides, progress became more and more difficult, and many travellers died, some falling into gulfs, others crushed by landslides, still others drowned in the whirlpools of mountain torrents which barred their path.

'On the morning of the next day, Burri stood high on the brink of an even deeper chasm, shouting a single word to the people: "Go!" before throwing himself over the edge.

'Without a word, Baikolla and Barguzzi dried their tears and led the people on until they could see the blue tips of mountains, much higher than those they had just crossed.

'Death cursed the courage of the brothers and took a very long time to come out of the abyss, but again it succeeded, and on the second night it caught up with the tribe.

'In the morning, before the eyes of the waking people, Barguzzi, without a word, threw himself into a chasm of immeasurable depth, in which nothing could be seen except floating tendrils of mist.

'The people walked without respite and climbed higher and higher.

'One fine morning, Baikolla, the last of the brothers, pointed forwards and said: "You will continue on your own. Find a valley and start a new life. I am going back to where my brothers are. We have done our best. If Death is still pursuing us, I shall confront it and drive it as far from you as I can."

'Without another word, Baikolla turned round and went back to meet Death. The people did not thank him, for there were no words great enough to express their gratitude. They continued their journey.

'The terrain they were crossing was becoming impassable and nowhere could the people see a valley which could support life. Finally, there rose in the people's path an immense ridge, quite covered in snow and ice, and the people fell to the ground in despair, for they no longer had the strength to scale the forbidding slopes of the ridge.

'Suddenly darkness fell all around, a deafening rumbling resounded and the people looked up to see a giant on the mountains. He stood above the ridge, snatching great clouds from out of the sky, smashing them together, bringing forth thunder and lightning.

'It was the valiant knight Sibir whose domain the people had entered in their search for the valley of life.

'The giant banged two immense clouds together and a spark fell into his eye. He began to rub it with his hand and sat down on top of the ridge which reached only as far as his knee. When he had finished rubbing his eye, he suddenly noticed the people on one of the slopes. He saw them and was amazed.

' "People!" he blared in his stentorian voice. "Why have you come into my land? There is no place to live here! There is nothing but stones and ice!"

'Although frightened by the giant's voice, the people told him the whole truth about themselves, about the death of thousands of their kin, and of the hunter brothers who had led them there and died to save them.

'There was no creature in the world stronger than the giant Sibir, but he was also benign. The troubles of the people moved him and he began to wonder what he could do. He drew himself up to his full gigantic height, looked all around him, but could think of nothing; then he looked down at his feet and saw a frozen ridge curved in the shape of a crescent. He bent down and, with only a slight effort, tore the ridge from the ground by the roots. He raised it above his head, looked to the north, the south, the east and the west, but there was nowhere to throw it – there were living things all around. He then spun the ridge round above his head and flung it into the heavens.

'The people saw the immense ridge disappear, and heard the valiant knight Sibir laughing with satisfaction. Where only a few moments before there had been an unassailable ridge, there was now a deep valley.

' "Live!" said the giant, in a huge, happy, joyful voice, and away he went, stepping over mountains and ridges.

'The people began to go down into the valley and the further they went the warmer it became; flowers blossomed on the mountainsides before their very eyes, crystal streams burst out of the stones, birds sang the song of life and wild animals, great and small, began running into the valley along the mountain terraces, overtaking the people.

'But the road was long and the people did not have time to go all the way down into the valley before night fell. When darkness came they were astonished to see in the heavens a shining crescent: it was the icy ridge thrown by the mighty hand of the giant Sibir; it shone in the sky, just as it does today . . . '

At this point in the story my face broke into an idiotic smile. The girl fell silent and gave me a look, full of surprise and reproof.

'Are you laughing? Why? Is it possible to laugh when the legend is being told?'

I attempted to justify myself: 'Oh no . . . it was just . . . the crescent moon isn't always there. The moon is sometimes round as a ball.'

'What of it?' replied the little girl, looking puzzled. 'In the Valley of the Young Moon there were very wise men who counted all the stars in the sky and could read men's futures in them. But that's a completely different matter. I'm telling you the legend, and every word of it is the truth, otherwise it wouldn't be the legend. The legend is the greatest truth of all.'

I didn't really understand what she was saying, but I deeply regretted my idiotic smile.

'Do please go on!' I begged.

'You must believe every word, otherwise you don't deserve to know the legend.'

'I do believe it! I swear I do!' I assured her hastily.

She was silent for a moment, collecting her thoughts. 'Years went by and the people swarmed all over the Valley of the Young Moon; that was what they called the valley of life given to the people by the valiant knight Sibir. The people divided into four tribes, each taking the name of one of the hunter brothers who had saved the people from the Black Death. In the north of the valley lived the Olkhonna tribe, famous for its countless herds of deer. The men of the Barguzzi tribe in the south were great hunters, while the Burri tribe in the east was renowned for its long-maned horses, capable of leaping wide, deep chasms. The Baikolla tribe in the south was recognised as the chief tribe and its prince, Baikolla, reigned over all the valley. Marvellous gardens flourished in the prince's land and his palace had no equal.

'None disturbed the peaceful life of the valley and all the weapons that the four tribes had preserved found a home for ever in one of the halls of Prince Baikolla's palace. Not once did hatred divide the tribes.'

The little girl fell silent and, when she looked at her father, sadness returned to her eyes.

'Did I tell the legend correctly, Father?'

He stroked her head lovingly and did not answer.

'You see before you the last prince of the Baikolla tribe and of the Valley of the Young Moon!' she murmured in a sad voice.

'But what happened then? Why was he the last?' I asked impatiently.

The little girl snuggled up to her father, looking somewhere beyond me, and I felt that my question caused her pain, but I had to know everything, otherwise there would be no sense in having come there. I could not shake off the presentiment that something in this story was to be changed because of me.

'Should I tell him, Father?' she asked in a choked voice.

'You may,' he replied gently.

'Then,' the little girl began, 'then, misfortune came . . . '

She stopped and closed her eyes; and when she reopened them, they shone with unshed tears.

'One day, after many, many years, a stranger came to the valley with her two sons. No one knew where she had come from, nor how she had found the way to the valley, nor why she was there; no one knew any of this and no one asked her, and she herself gave nothing away. There was plenty of land available in the valley, the woman was not disturbing anyone and nobody disturbed her. She settled down with her sons, isolated from the tribe, visiting no one and making no one's acquaintance.

'She was very tall, even taller than the tallest men in the valley, and her sons . . . '

At this point in the story the little girl fell silent again and closed her eyes.

'I . . . I can't go on. I'm weary,' she said.

'She's weary,' Baikolla repeated.

Although this was not an order, I understood that I ought to leave, which meant I would learn no more that day. As for another day, I would just have to go on living until then . . .

I said goodbye and, not receiving any answer, drifted off slowly towards the stairs leading to the rooms above.

The sight of the sparkling weapons on the walls no longer afforded me any pleasure. Mechanically I put my hand on a long pointed lance, sat down on a bear-skin and lay on my back for what seemed a long time, hearing the voice of Prince Baikolla's daughter recounting the legend. I also endeavoured to understand how the legend could be the truth, since the facts it recounted had never taken place. But one didn't find old women dressed in blue on the top of crags, and yet, up there, in front of the stone commanding the entrance to the castle, sat old Sarma – that was a fact! But if I were to relate that fact to someone who had not seen it with his own eyes, would he believe me?

Supposing I tried to ask Sarma the end of the legend? I still did not know the name of the young girl. She hadn't asked mine, and I had not dared inquire about hers; besides, the opportunity had not arisen.

I leapt up the steps four at a time, raced through the cave and a minute later I was with Sarma. She greeted me with abuse: 'And who's going to close the entrance behind you, squeaking little grasshopper?'

I went back and pushed the stone. Sarma's voice, hideous as ever, chilled me, and I gave up the idea of asking her anything. I went up to the old woman and sat down beside her on the stone. She squinted at me suspiciously, clicked her lips, but said nothing. When I looked up at her a minute later her face was as sad as it had been on my previous visit, and as before my hostility melted away instantly.

I plunged in: 'Grandmother,' I said simply, in a perfectly relaxed tone of voice, 'they told me the legend in there, so now I know how it all was . . . I mean, how it all began . . . Since I know that, maybe you could tell me the end of the legend, why they're down there . . . and you . . . why you're sitting here . . .'

I really had no desire to be told off again; I so badly wanted to hear her talking normally. And that was what she did. Without turning towards me, she asked, without her usual sarcasm: 'Why didn't they tell you everything?'

'The little girl wanted to, but she couldn't go on . . . She was weary.'

A vengeful expression flickered on Sarma's face and reverberated in her answer: 'Of course! It's always difficult to tell of a crime.'

'You'll tell me the rest, won't you?' I begged.

Sarma's look became haughty, making her seem not so very old after all. 'You want to know why I'm here? Look in front of you. What do you see?'

In front of me, framed in the triangle of a gorge, Baikal unfolded itself to my gaze, and when I answered 'Baikal', I relived anew the beauty of the view that opened up from the crag.

'Please, don't mangle names. I can't bear it!' she said, and her face became a mass of lines. 'You don't see, and you can't see. Deep down, at the very bottom of the lake, where the fish don't venture, there rests a marble coffin and in that coffin lies my beloved younger son Marit.'

She fell silent, and I did not dare ask her to hurry.

'When I went with my sons into the Valley of the Young Moon, I knew where I was going and why I was going. But I said nothing to the people of the valley. They were to find out everything later . . . '

Sarma sighed. 'Perhaps I should have told them everything; then perhaps none of it would have happened . . .

'My elder son – his name was Nessei – was seventeen years old, but he was already a grown man, and none of the men of the valley could match him in strength, intelligence or skill. The very strongest men of the valley looked like youths beside him. Marit, my younger son . . . he was ten, but he could bring down a bird with a single stone, pull the string of the tallest bow and subdue the most restive horse of the Burri tribe. Yes . . . such were my sons!

'Now, at that time, the eldest daughter of Prince Baikolla celebrated her sixteenth birthday; the astrologers read her name in the stars and called her Ngara, meaning "Quick Eye". The astrologers of the valley knew what they were about; for she did indeed have a quick eye. She set her heart on my son Nessei and lured him to her. My eyes were not as quick as hers and I did not notice their love.

'One day out of the blue, Nessei told me he wanted to marry Prince Baikolla's daughter. I tried to talk him out of it, or to persuade him to wait, but my son was a man and would neither wait nor try to understand me.

'So I went to find the Prince of the Valley and announced that my son wanted to marry his daughter. Oh no! I didn't ask him to give his daughter in marriage to my son. I told him proudly that my son wanted to marry his daughter and that he, Prince Baikolla, should take pride in my intercession.

'Who was I to the Prince? A woman of no family, a stranger in the valley, belonging to no tribe. Now, according to custom, marriages through the ages had cemented the friendship between tribes of the Valley of the Young Moon. I replied to Prince Baikolla's silence with impertinence. Yes, impertinence! Because it was justified.

'I said to him: "Why are you taking so long, Prince? Why do you not hurry to announce the betrothal to the elders? Why do you not offer me a place at your side?"

'Prince Baikolla had never raised his voice to anyone. Nor did he on this occasion. He answered quietly, between clenched teeth: "Go away, woman! I bear you no ill will, but henceforward I shall not invite you to my castle."

'He could not say anything else to me. He knew who I was.

' "You will regret it, Prince!" I replied, and left.

'There was a particular custom in the Valley of the Young Moon: when someone came on foot to petition the Prince, he would go home on a horse given by the Prince – no matter what answer was received.

'They brought my horse to the palace gate, but I refused to take it and went home on foot. I walked through the lands of Baikolla, and the lands of Burri, and the people of the Barguzzi tribe saw me returning on foot from the castle of Baikolla. There could have been no greater affront to the Prince of the Valley!

'When I broke the news of Baikolla's refusal to my son Nessei, he smashed his bow on the ground in fury. I begged him not to be distressed, and told him the day would come when Prince Baikolla himself would walk to our home to request the honour of an alliance with us. I knew what I was saying. But my son decided otherwise.

'Through the mediation of Baikolla's younger daughter, the one you have seen in the castle – she was only eleven and did not yet have her real name, she was simply known as Ri, meaning "Prince's daughter" – Nessei established contact with Ngara and suggested she should elope with him. And, of course, the girl agreed. What girl of the valley would have refused my son anything?

'When night fell, my two sons rode stealthily to Baikolla's castle and Ri led her sister to the appointed place. Nessei lifted her up on to the saddle and they galloped away from the castle.

'But my younger son, my Marit, felt himself to be a man as well, and did not want to be left out. He grabbed Baikolla's younger daughter, sat her on the saddle in front of him and galloped off after his brother.

'Oh, if only I had foreseen this terrible misfortune, I could have saved my son! I knew how to get out of the valley. But my sons did not. On the winged chargers of the Burri tribe, they galloped right to the foot of the mountains, but nowhere could they find the path that would save them.

'In the morning, as I was putting on my finest attire to visit the people of the valley and tell them about myself, Baikolla's men at that very moment were galloping on the heels of my sons whom they had managed to separate. Word of what was happening had already reached me and I flew to the aid of my sons. By means of a secret power I was able to open up a passage in the mountain for Nessei, just as his enemies were about to capture him.

'But I could not help my younger son. Baikolla's men had driven him to the brink of an abyss which even the most valiant knights of the valley would not have risked leaping over. But my young son, my Marit, was braver than any of the men of the valley; he spurred on his mount and hurled himself across the abyss, and he would have crossed it had Prince Baikolla not drawn his bow. The arrow hit the horse in the neck and, just as he was crossing the abyss, his strength failed him and only his front hooves touched the far side of the precipice.

'And then . . . are you listening, boy? Then my son could still have saved his own life. But he was a man of honour and he just had time to set down his captive, Baikolla's daughter, on a rocky ledge. As for him . . . he plunged to the bottom of the abyss alone, with his horse.'

Sarma's voice trembled, and I, too, could feel a lump in my throat which impeded my listening to the old woman.

'Murder had never been committed in the Valley of the Young Moon, and after Baikolla had killed Marit, the people were frozen with horror and stood in painful silence on the edge of the precipice until I arrived at the place where my son had perished.

'How great was my grief! Who can understand it! Only those who have lost a son!

'And my anger! Who *cannot* understand it! Those who have not known grief!

'Leaning over the precipice, I said to the people of the valley: "Listen, and know the extent of your crime. You have killed the descendant of the valiant knight Sibir, who gave you the valley of life. I had come here to save you. Savage peoples are on their way to the valley and you will not have the strength to defend your freedom. I brought my valiant sons to you; we wanted to help you, but you have decided your own fate. Grieve!"

'The people of the valley fell on their knees; only Prince Baikolla and his daughter remained standing, for they

91

understood their sin and knew it would not be forgiven. They stood before me as though before a court of justice.

'I ordered them to go to the castle and await my decision. I commanded the people to lay the body of my son in a marble coffin and carry it to the lowest point of the valley. I gave the people time to prepare themselves and showed them a safe path leading out of the valley. Then, exercising the power bequeathed to me by the heirs of the giant Sibir, I trampled on the ice which covered the summits of the blue mountains, and the water gushed into the valley and flooded it: it became the valley of the tomb of my son Marit.

'The heirs of Sibir had further entrusted me with the secret of eternal life and everlasting youth, which meant that my grief, too, would be eternal. The punishment for those responsible for my son's death is that of eternal repentance. That is a just punishment. Who would dare claim that it is not?'

We watched each other in silence for a long time. Now I knew everything, but that did not mean I understood it all.

'But what had Ri done wrong?' I asked, collecting my thoughts at last.

'Wrong?' exclaimed Sarma. 'Wasn't she the cause of it all? Wasn't it saving her life that cost my son his?'

No, this I didn't understand.

'But look, so many years have gone by,' I answered. 'Why won't you forgive them?'

'Don't dare,' squeaked the old woman. 'Don't ever dare to say the word "forgive". It doesn't exist. Remember this: it's only those who can't avenge themselves who forgive. I can avenge myself. And my vengeance is sacred, it is eternal, as my sorrow is eternal. Forgive? Do you think forgiveness will bring my son back out of his tomb? Forgiveness is the lie told by the weak heart.'

'That's not true!' I exclaimed. 'Mother has forgiven me lots of times when I've done something wrong.'

'You!' said Sarma, with a scornful sneer. 'Why should anyone forgive you, or not forgive you? You've known nothing yet in life, neither evil nor good. You're not a man yet, you're just a little greenhorn. For the moment it's your parents who have to account for their actions. Why, you're just a little grasshopper! Why take it on yourself to pass judgement? Spare your head the trouble!'

Where did she get this obsession with giving offence at all costs? I was used to it by now, however, and tried not to take any notice.

'Remember,' she continued in her haughty tone, 'remember, even though you can't understand. The person who has most need of forgiveness is he who forgives, because the burden of vengeance is too heavy and painful for him. But revenge is a duty. To forgive is to betray one's duty. If evil is not punished it will come to pass for good, and that will signal the end of everything. Good is memorable for good. The memory of evil resides in its punishment. If you want to be a man, never ask forgiveness and never forgive anybody.'

'That's not fair,' I muttered between my teeth, for I didn't want her to hear me. But she caught the words and was stupefied.

'You have the effrontery to argue with me. If you don't watch out, I'll send you down the crag head-first, little jackal!'

I was almost frightened, but hit on a splendid reply: 'In that case, my father will spend his life avenging me.'

The old woman blinked her white eyelashes in surprise, momentarily struck dumb. 'Go away,' she hissed at last, 'and never dare to show your face here again!'

That was when I got thoroughly scared. I had to keep coming back. I almost asked her to forgive me, but remembered what she thought of that word.

'I'll never say that again. I won't argue with you any more, promise.'

'What do you know about promises, filthy little prattler?' she said with her usual scorn, though slightly softer and less nasty. I decided this was enough for one day; I ought to leave before our relationship was permanently damaged.

'Goodbye,' I said as politely as possible.

Sarma did not answer.

On my way down the crag I lingered for a long time on a ledge to contemplate the vast expanse of Lake Baikal before my eyes, the shores of navy blue rising towards the sky and the light blue of the sky dipping into the water.

So, once upon a time, there had been no lake here. There had been a valley where people lived, gardens flourished, flocks grazed; now there was a splendid expanse of water, full of surprises, a lake whose very name commemorated the hero of the legend of the Valley of the Young Moon. And here inside the crag was the last prince of that enchanted country, a land which had disappeared beneath the water without any trace other than a consonance in the names of winds, villages and islands.

But what was the use of concentrating on irrevocable events? Better to think of what I could do on behalf of the captives in Dead Man's Crag. I needed to understand everything down to the minutest detail of this sad story and not leave it to the ingenuous impulses of the spirit. The people of the Valley of the Young Moon understood many things differently from us. I still did not understand everything and there were perhaps some points in the behaviour and thoughts of Sarma and her captives that I was not granted to understand, but that in no way meant I should stand around and do nothing.

About three hundred metres from the last house in the village I saw several boys standing in a circle at the side of the road. They were discussing something heatedly or having some kind of quarrel as I approached. From behind Valerka I could see Yurka holding a stick with a pitchfork at the end and pinning down the head of a huge adder. The snake was flailing about on the ground, thrashing at the stick and coiling around it, powerless to extricate itself. The boys parted to let me see the adder clearly. I had never seen such a big one, but not wishing to go unduly close, I preferred to be horrified from a distance.

'It was a snake like this that bit me last year!' Yurka announced proudly. All the boys looked enviously at Yurka, and then at the snake.

'What are you going to do with it?' I asked.

'What am I going to do with it? We're going to take it to the ant-heap straight away and the ants will eat it alive. You'll see, there won't be the tiniest little bone left.'

Suddenly a voice spoke behind me. 'Why are you tormenting that creature? You should let it go.'

I turned round and stood rooted to the spot in amazement. Sarma was standing beside me. Admittedly she was dressed quite normally and wasn't wearing her blue robe, and her voice was slightly different too. But could two old women look so alike? For a second I wondered how she could have got down from the crag so fast and when she had found time to change, but I dismissed these stupid questions at once. For Sarma, that was mere child's play.

'You ought to let it go,' she repeated to Yurka.

This request aroused general indignation. That was all we needed! To feel sorry for an adder!

'And then the bastard will bite somebody else. I won't let it go!'

Yurka's mouth was set in an obstinate line. Nobody seemed surprised by the old woman's arrival.

I nudged Valerka in the ribs. 'Who is she?'

'Old Vassina. A witch. Last year when the adder bit Yurka she whispered some magic words. You should have seen how his hand was swollen!'

Old Vassina. That was who she was, though I certainly had thought it was Sarma to begin with. There was definitely a resemblance, but only slight. The main thing was, would Sarma have felt sorry for a snake? Definitely not!

'Maybe it was this filthy beast that bit me last year,' said Yurka malevolently, leaning harder on the stick.

'It didn't do it on purpose,' replied old Vassina calmly. 'You were picking wild berries, you reached out your hand and the snake thought you meant to hurt it, so it bit you. It didn't set out to attack you.'

'So, I don't even have the right to pick berries now!'

'Why shouldn't you have the right? Of course you have. But the snake also has a right to defend itself. You ought to let it go.'

Yurka gave a nasty snort. But old Vassina's authority was great. Looking at Yurka, she said with a smile: 'Perhaps it will never bite anyone again. And if it does, I'll cure the victim very quickly, you'll see. I'll whisper a few magic words and that'll do the trick.'

'Should I let it go then?' said Yurka, beginning to capitulate.

The boys, including me, started to protest vehemently.

'Move away!' he cried. 'I'm letting it go.'

Everyone scattered, only Vassina stayed where she was. Sensing its freedom, the adder wound its way jerkily as far as the stones; when it got there it turned its head and gave such a menacing hiss that I felt a shiver down my back.

'It's saying thank you,' said old Vassina to Yurka.

'I heard that thank you in my grave,' muttered Yurka, a sentiment I shared completely.

The boys, disappointed and even angry, moved away towards the village; I lagged behind without being noticed and went back to the scene of the drama, hoping to find the old woman. Her resemblance to Sarma worried me a great deal.

Not finding her there, I went on towards the gorge where I soon saw her. She was picking something from the bushes near the stream. As I stole up on her I realised she was gathering some kind of herb, but I didn't have time to see which before she turned round and saw me.

'Do you want to know what I'm looking for?' she asked.

I nodded.

'Well, look, this herb cures indigestion.'

'How do you know?'

'I just know.' She smiled.

'Will you let me help you?'

'Look around then, look around!' she said.

There was no need to look far. In a minute I had picked

a whole clump which I gave to her. She sorted it out sprig by sprig, put two of them in her bag and handed me back the rest. 'Those aren't the right kind!'

'Why not?' I asked in surprise.

'Look,' she said, taking the sprigs out of her bag, 'they're absolutely identical, aren't they?'

'Yes,' I said with a shrug.

'You see the little pimples on the stem? That's where all its strength is. The herb without pimples is a false herb.'

'Why's that?'

The old woman sat down on a tussock of earth, opened her bag and began to pick over the herbs, spreading them out in clumps. 'The good, health-giving herb grows, and its value is great. Another plant springs up and wants to be equally valued. So it imitates the good herb, same size, same colour, everything the same. But those pimples on the stem don't look nice. That's what the false herb thinks. How can a smooth stem possibly make any difference? And yet it's the stem that shows it to be an imposter.'

'And what else?' I asked, eager to hear more from this strange old woman.

'There's also, for instance, the false mushroom. To look at, it's a real orange-cap boletus. But if you break it, the inside immediately starts to turn black with annoyance because its falseness has been exposed.'

'And is there such a thing as a false person?'

'Oh yes, there certainly is!' she replied calmly.

'How do you recognise him?'

'Unless he's deceived you, it's absolutely impossible.'

'But that's not fair,' I protested.

Old Vassina inclined her head vaguely. 'Well, let him trick you. So what? The deceit will stay in him, it won't follow you. The person a bad man hurts most is himself; being bad harms him more than it does others.'

It's not like that at all, I thought. If a snake were to bite me, how could it hurt the snake more than me? The old woman could go and tell her fairy-tales to someone else.

'Whose son are you? I can't place you.'

'We haven't been here very long.'

'So you're the schoolteachers' son?'

I nodded.

'Well, if anything goes wrong, if you have toothache or a stomachache, come and find me. It can't do you any harm.'

'I'll come,' I promised, hoping the opportunity wouldn't arise.

'This evening I'm going a long way away. Don't follow me,' she said, getting up from her tussock.

In any case, I had to go home. I took my leave of old Vassina and set off for the village.

During the evening I found the atlas and eagerly studied the map of Lake Baikal until I came across the familiar names: Olkhon, Barguzin, Angara, Yenissei . . . How strangely the history of Baikal was preserved in the human memory: 'Angara, the daughter of Baikal, eloped with the handsome Yenissei.' Everyone thought it was only a fairy-tale, never suspecting the existence of the valiant young knight Nessei, nor of Ngara, daughter of Prince Baikolla; they had no idea that the fairy-tale concealed the true story of the Valley of the Young Moon.

On the map Lake Baikal resembled the shape of a crescent moon and although that night there was a full moon in the sky, as round as a football, it still seemed too much of a coincidence.

Once again the eyes of Baikolla's daughter appeared

before me, the eyes of a child with no name, known simply as Ri. I tried to grasp how she could be in the wrong in Sarma's eyes, but I couldn't understand the old woman. I was more and more certain that Sarma had an equal share in any guilt, even though she had lost her son.

In the room facing, Mother was sitting at her desk writing something in the lamplight. I walked up to the door and leant against the jamb.

'What do you want?' Mother asked, continuing to write.

'Mama, how do people forgive each other?'

'How do they forgive each other? Well, they forgive each other, that's all.'

She went on writing, without turning round.

'Well, suppose somebody's guilty of some wicked act, and you forgive them, that means you forget the thing they did wrong, is that right?'

Mama looked at me but she was evidently still thinking about her work and answered me mechanically: 'Maybe you forget it at some point. Can't you see I'm busy?'

But I needed to clear up the problem completely, once and for all. 'Mama, when you forgive somebody, what becomes of the guilt?'

She laid down her pen and turned towards me. 'What stupid questions you're asking!'

'Well, listen, if somebody killed me, would you forgive them?'

'What nonsense you're talking! Whoever's thinking of killing you?' Mother was beginning to get angry.

'No one, but supposing somebody did? Would you forgive them?'

'No, I wouldn't!'

'And what if they were miserable and they repented for years and years, would you forgive them?'

Mother gave me a suspicious look. 'You've done something silly today, is that it? Admit it!'

'I haven't done anything, I just need to know.'

Mother cleared away the books from the other chair and called me over: 'Come and sit here.'

'After many, many years, would you forgive them?'

'I don't know,' she said, after pausing for thought. 'Maybe not.'

'You remember when I broke the gramophone? You wouldn't let me go out afterwards. Then in the evening I asked you to forgive me, and you forgave me. Why?'

'Because you hadn't done it on purpose.'

'In that case, why did you say I couldn't go out?'

'Oh my goodness!' laughed my mother. 'After all, you did break the gramophone.'

I thought very hard. 'Yes, and afterwards we had to do without a gramophone. But you forgave me. Why?'

'I don't understand what you're getting at. Later on we bought a radiogram. That was better than a gramophone, wasn't it?'

'Mama,' I said, trying to explain clearly, 'the gramophone was beyond repair, it had ceased to exist. That means I'm guilty towards it for the rest of my life, doesn't it?'

'Guilty towards whom?' asked my mother, frowning and losing patience.

'The gramophone!'

Mama felt my forehead and looked anxiously at me. 'Are you ill, or are you just acting the fool?'

'But please understand, Mama, that time you said "I forgive you", the gramophone went on being broken. And after you'd forgiven me it didn't get mended and it didn't start playing again. How could you forgive me if nothing had been put right?'

'Why are you getting everything muddled?' asked my mother, her brow growing even darker. 'You were careless and you broke the gramophone. To punish you, I kept you in. You apologised, I forgave you. What more is there to say?'

'And why did I apologise?'

'This is getting more and more complicated. Didn't you feel guilty?'

'But after you'd forgiven me, did I stop being guilty? I did? But the gramophone didn't get better.'

Mother lost her patience and took me by the hand.

'Do please wait, Mama,' I begged. 'Wait, I don't understand. You didn't let me go out, and that was some kind of revenge, wasn't it?'

'What are you on about?'

I had obviously driven my mother to her wit's end and ought to have ended the discussion there; but I was unable to stop myself and headed straight for an argument.

'If I was guilty towards the gramophone, you had to take revenge on me in its name, that's the law, isn't it?'

Without a word, Mother took my hand and led me into my bedroom, up to my bed, and issued an order: 'In ten minutes' time you've got to be asleep.'

Ten minutes later, strange as it might seem, I do believe I was asleep.

4

I N ALL COUNTRIES where the winter is harsh, summer brings a reign of joy. More often than not it is simply the best season of the year. I lived in the north where summer is like a gift from heaven. But it is ephemeral; the two months pass in a flash and then nature resumes its true face, the essence of which is snow and freezing cold.

On Baikal summer embodies all the aims and objectives of nature . . . Nature is always preparing for summer, and each raging blizzard, each fall of snow, each winter gale and spring wind – all are given sense and significance by summer.

In the faded white of winter the colours of the water in Baikal accumulate, mature and ripen. Only an extremely subtle artist would be able to give a name to each nuance of the waves, but even he would be unable to transpose them to his canvas, because his brush is capable of catching only a fleeting moment of nature. The colour of the water is its true life, not characterised by any of its ephemeral appearances, however brilliant. That is why the canvas of the most gifted artist will be only a photograph of the briefest moments, which exist in reality by the thousand, each more beautiful than the last and each of which contributes equally to the essence of Baikal.

Summer on Baikal is a joy. Not only the spiritual joy we feel as a consequence of summer, but a joy in itself. This joy is all around: it lives in the warmth of the stone baked by the sun, in the cool splash of the waves, in the fragrant bouquet from the mountains, where countless flowers and shrubs blossom, and in the call of the gulls above the sandbanks; above all, joy comes from the fact that you live in such a wondrous part of the world, in perfect communion with the surrounding beauty.

None of life's burdens can resist this joy. It works its way into the heart, just as the ray of afternoon summer sunlight strikes through the thick forest, and into the most secret corners of the gorges, where the flowers, like raspberry-coloured velvet, blossom among the damp shadows.

The sad secret of Dead Man's Crag had polarised all my emotions and feelings. Nevertheless, every day, before I went to the gorge, I would run to the beach and swim and dive with the other boys. I was becoming involved in swimming contests at greater and greater distances from the shore, took part in the most acrobatic diving, and did not flinch from playing water 'chase', floating on railway sleepers and rafts, or joining in all the other aquatic pranks.

Sometimes I would climb the mountains with the boys, clambering up to the highest summits, and in the little crevasses at the top we would pick wild cherries, a unique delicacy of the Siberian taiga.

I climbed trees wherever I could, particularly cedars, to pick their delicate resinous cones; but often I would scale silver birches, struggling to the very top for the sheer pleasure of 'parachuting down', thereby risking a broken leg on the stones or roots below.

Stones would often hurtle down the mountains, causing landslides, and I took a wild delight in watching them fly down in a series of crashing explosions, bouncing into the air when they struck the furthest ledges, and finally plunging into the water, raising splashes like clouds of crystal splinters.

No matter how deeply I was involved in any game, however, the moment always came when my eyes would turn towards Dead Man's Crag; and then I would drop everything, tearing into the gorge to climb the crag.

Virtually the same pattern would be repeated on each occasion: I would greet Sarma, whose whole demeanour demonstrated how tired she was of me, and the distaste she felt for me. I would hover around her for a few minutes, then she would say irritably: 'Well, what you are hanging around here for, you haven't come to see me!'

'Can I go in, then?' I would ask and, not receiving any answer, would go to the stone, move it and race into the half-darkness of the cave.

They were no longer surprised to see me in the hall of pillars, and I think Ri even enjoyed my visits, although, to tell the truth, when I looked into her eyes, there was a total absence of joy. It was actually as if her eyes were completely incapable of accommodating such an emotion. Sometimes a flash of life would appear in them, when she was telling me, for example, about the beauty of her elder sister Ngara, or about the celebrations held in the Valley of the Young Moon, the jousting tournaments between the young men, or again when she was describing the beauty of the valley on a lovely sunny day. But as soon as she stopped talking, the light in her eyes went out, and then I was lashed by pity bordering on despair.

Prince Baikolla hardly ever joined in the conversations. Usually he simply sat gazing at his daughter, his eyes overflowing with love and pity, even when he closed them to stop himself crying.

To be frank, I too found that listening to Ri was always painful. But it was even more painful to describe my life, and our life in general, when she asked me to. There were many things she couldn't understand or was amazed by, and I often caught myself trying to give uninteresting accounts of our life because the interest she took in what went on outside the stone walls of the castle could only accentuate the grief of her captivity.

For my part, I knew only one thing: I must set her free, I must save her, even if she were the only one. I felt no longer as concerned with Baikolla, nor even with the little dog, the silent participant in our conversations, whose sad appearance could have aroused pity in the hardest of hearts.

Only Sarma, fossilised in her throne of rock, refused to listen to any suggestion of forgiving her captives. I had already given up mentioning it to her. Now I determined to discuss escape with Baikolla and his daughter. I had already tried to broach the subject several times, but each time Baikolla remained silent, Ri sadly shook her head, and only once, when I had been too insistent, Baikolla had said: 'My daughter has told you the legend and you know the price and the miracle by which our people won the valley of life. I am not only guilty of the death of Sarma's son; for her, that death is her single sorrow; but I suffer more cruelly from the destruction of the valley and all the certain ills my people had to endure when they left these parts. I thank the stars I remain ignorant of those!'

'But what about Ri!' I exclaimed. 'What has it to do with her? Why is she here?'

Baikolla's brow grew darker still. 'For no reason! She is the measure of my punishment!'

'It's all Sarma's fault. She doesn't understand anything about anything, evil, destructive old woman!' I cried, banging my fist on the ground.

'Old woman?' asked Baikolla. 'Who are you talking about?'

'Sarma! Who else?'

'Has she grown old? Surely not. She knew the secret of eternal youth.'

I shrugged. 'She's as old and hideous as a hundred of the oldest, most repulsive women all rolled together.'

Baikolla lapsed into thought and shook his head. 'So, her grief has turned out stronger than eternal youth.'

'Maybe her malice, not her grief,' I muttered.

'It isn't right to talk like that,' Ri reproached me.

I began to grind my teeth with anger. Sarma deprived her of the happiness of living, and Ri was defending her.

That day I emerged from the castle more angry with Sarma than usual. When I got back to the top, I longed to say something insulting, so I asked, as casually as possible: 'Baikolla was telling me you knew the secret of eternal youth, so how is it you've got so old?'

'Old?' she gasped. 'You say I'm old?'

The blue-gloved hand darted forward and a small round mirror appeared in it. The old woman looked at herself, her eyes widened, she held the mirror close to her face, her mouth gaped; her face, which was already frightening to behold, contorted, her whole body trembled, and suddenly, with a violent gesture, she hurled the mirror against the side of the crag, which immediately subsided like a snowdrift and in the same moment crashed into the gorge below.

Sarma leapt from her throne and gave such an appalling shriek that my hair stood on end. She threw back her blue hood and put her hand into her snow-white hair. Then she tore the blue glove from her hand, stared insanely at the yellow phalanxes of her fingers, and began to shriek once more, fearsomely and savagely, while all around her the stones were rolling and hurtling down the mountain. A cloud of dust rose above the crag, and in its midst the old woman in blue screamed and gesticulated.

I was seized by such terror that my legs carried me of their own volition down the crag and, paying no attention to the stones breaking away from the ledges, or to the din of the veritable landslide going on just two metres away from me, I took to my heels, throwing caution to the winds, and practically rolled down the crag to escape from Sarma's frenzied cries.

It was when I reached the bottom, below the crag itself, that something struck me on the head and I was purely and simply switched off from the whole nightmare.

The most infuriating moment of the whole episode was when Genka maintained I was shouting with fear at the sight of the landslide. Of course I couldn't explain that it wasn't me at all, but Sarma who was screaming. Besides, who would have believed such a story?

Genka and his grandfather had been coming back from the taiga with a sledge full of hay when they heard the landslide and the shouts. They found me at the bottom of Dead Man's Crag, my head split open and soaked in blood – so much blood that at first they thought I was already dead. They took me to the village clinic which was right on the shore of Baikal, and the first thing I heard when I came round was the sound of waves through the open window. Then, I don't know why, I saw Genka's grandfather and thought it was Baikolla, because Grandad had the same white beard and his eyes had a melancholy expression similar to the eternal grief in Baikolla's eyes. I stared at

Grandad for a long time, and though my head ached and buzzed, I still realised that this was not Baikolla, so the fatal question did not pass my lips after all.

Then, an unfamiliar face appeared in front of Grandad's and only when I saw the white coat did I guess I was in hospital. I tried to move, but the pain in my head made me cry out, and immediately several people swam about before my eyes; I didn't pass out completely, but became indifferent to everything, and when first my mother, and soon afterwards my father, appeared among the shadows flitting around me, my state of apathy was a genuine blessing, for there is no greater torment that seeing one's own mother crying and wailing.

The stone had hit me flat on the back of the head, and it was to this stroke of luck that I owed my life.

Once again, the days in bed dragged out. Genka the boatman came to visit me more often than the others. He really considered himself something of a hero, and couldn't stop talking about how he and his grandfather had found me, how the stones were flying about and how I was shouting my head off . . . The way he described my screams made me furious, but I understood how he felt: it wasn't every day that a landslide happened on Dead Man's Crag, or that a villager was caught underneath it.

Valerka and Yurka also came to see me, and so did Svetka, who brought me bilberries, and her father, who told my father some barely comprehensible story about Genka's grandfather, known apparently in the village as White Grandad, on account of his beard. I was only half listening to this story, though when I caught the name of old Vassina I got interested, but by then they were already talking about something else. The bilberry season had arrived and my friends from the village came to see me with their lips and tongues stained purple. They had had their faces eaten alive by mosquitoes because the bilberries only grew in the little depressions which were the natural habitat of mosquitoes in the Siberian taiga.

As soon as I was left alone, however, my thoughts immediately returned to the rocky platform of Dead Man's Crag, where I would once again see Sarma's face, contorted with horror, and her aged hand with the knotted fingers spread out. I would hear the din of the landslide which at once revived the state of panic which had sent me hurtling down the crag in flight from the screeches of an old woman who had thought she was young.

I could now understand her flashy garb, her affectations, her gestures; she acted as if she were a young and attractive woman, that was why she was made ridiculous and repulsive by her simpering grimaces.

But what would happen now? Would she let me into the castle any more?

Deep down I was certain that my adventure was not yet over, because an ending like this was not possible, and because it would have been hard to understand why it had begun in the first place . . .

I was recovering quite quickly. The wound in my head was not deep, everything else was proceeding normally, and every morning I felt as if I could have leapt out of bed and gone running either to Baikal or into the drop, but the first abrupt movement registered an appreciable pain in my head which had an immediate sobering effect.

A few days later, however, there I was, with a bandaged head, sitting on a tall flat rock by the shore, hugging my knees, listening to the sound of the waves and watching them run on to the stone just below my feet, not too fast, not too noisily. The Barguzin that day was languid and sluggish, only a distant echo of the storm of the previous night, and even the splashes didn't reach the top of the rock I was sitting on.

The day was murky and the waves light grey. But now and then the sun would break through the gaps in the clouds, and although I had my back to it, I guessed it was going to appear long before it did, for the waves suddenly began to take on a blue tinge, and the sandbank to my right glistened.

I caught myself smiling for no particular reason as soon as the waves turned blue, and guessed that the smile on my face was somehow a response, as you smile at someone who has smiled at you. And then I understood that the blue of Baikal's water was its smile. In fact when the waves turned grey again, my own spirits immediately turned serious, even sad, and I felt like sighing, as one does when tired or bored.

Then Genka arrived in his boat and we spent a long time simply rocking on the waves, about a hundred metres from the shoreline. Genka was worried. His grandfather had fallen ill; this was the man who had taken me to the clinic and who was nicknamed White Grandad in the village. Genka told me how they used to go fishing together, or gathering cones, or even hunting, and although Genka was not actually assuming the worst, I sensed from the way he spoke that he feared for his grandfather's life.

A few days later, I found myself at the foot of Dead Man's Crag, but my legs rebelled against taking the first steps of the climb. I wandered around the crag for a long time, sometimes moving away altogether and scrambling up the slope of the gorge instead. I did not even notice that I had somehow managed to pick a bunch of flowers. It would be most awkward and tiresome to climb the crag carrying that; none the less I set off, holding my flowers . . .

Before I reached the final ledge, I held my breath and pricked up my ears, unable to make up my mind to take the last step. Who could tell what welcome Sarma was saving up for me?

Suddenly I heard her voice: 'Well, why are you hiding?'

I started, and recoiled, trying to decide her state of mind from the sound of her voice. But there was no sense in staying hidden. I went up on to the ledge.

At first glance it seemed as if Sarma was not in her usual place. That was because I was accustomed to her sky-blue clothes. Now she was dressed entirely in grey-brown, matching the colour of the rocks; she was even difficult to pick out because her face was grey, so that she seemed altogether blended into the colour of the stones.

I must have been staring at her – or at the very least looking in her direction – since she muttered irritably: 'What are you gaping at? Don't you dare look at me like that.'

Bewildered, I rolled my eyes.

'I know I'm a terrible sight,' she whispered. 'Perhaps I'll die, and that would be lucky!'

'Oh, come, that's no way to talk,' I said, for the sake of saying something.

'Yes, lucky!' she repeated, louder. 'Lucky for everyone. And for them too!'

I understood who she meant and I felt ashamed and disgusted because I almost agreed with her; to erase my unexpected guilt, I took a step towards her and dropped the flowers in her lap.

She threw them to the ground, as though they were not flowers at all, but a toad covered with warts.

'Don't dare pity me. You're nothing but a miserable little runt. Sarma doesn't need pity. Go to the people you've come to see. Go on!'

I rushed to the stone but Sarma called me back, and said in a completely different voice: 'Pick up your flowers. The people you brought them for need them more than I do.'

'Thank you!' I cried joyfully, and gathering up every last one of the flowers, I ran to the castle entrance.

How glad Baikolla's daughter was to see the flowers: 'Father!' she whispered excitedly, 'look, these are flowers from the valley! They used to grow round the castle and Ngara made wreaths out of them for the victors of the tournaments.'

She began to say the names of the flowers, and, very strangely, they were called exactly the same in the Valley of the Young Moon: cuckoo-boats, cuckoo-tears, iris, and fire-flowers. Ri sorted them out by colour and smiled at each of them; these were her very first smiles, and it would have been better if I hadn't seen them . . .

I had a feeling that Baikolla was looking at me reprovingly. He was right, of course. I was really torturing the little girl by evoking her thirst for life and thus condemning her to even greater suffering.

But what was I to do? Leave them there and never come back? That I found quite impossible. I could not release them because they themselves did not want to be set free; besides, Sarma would surely have foreseen any such attempt on my part.

It would have been perfectly true to say that I was

suffering, but in that case my sufferings were simply absurd compared to those of Ri, and to those of the Prince himself.

Every time I went home, I constructed plans, each one more fantastic than the other. To begin with, all my plans were based on a course of events which would involve one or more outsiders in the affair. It seemed to me then that if somebody else, or a few other people, or indeed everyone, knew my secret, the fate of the captives of Dead Man's Crag could have been settled.

But the more I thought about the whole business, the clearer it became that no one single-handedly, no group of people collectively, could put an end to the cruel absurdity of the secret; it was not strength or numbers that could save those two people who had become so dear to me. I sometimes felt that not only Ri and her father, but Sarma as well, were expecting something of me, even though I was only a boy; I thought many a time, for instance, that Sarma was weary of her vengeance and her grief, that Baikolla was counting on me and that Ri secretly did not believe she was going to survive.

When all these ideas struck me, I would try to encourage Sarma to speak openly, striving to be as polite as possible to her, but she seemed to demand that I shouldn't involve her in my secret thoughts, and was not inclined to help me in any way.

It was during this time that my relationship with Sarma changed completely. My loathing for her was such that it quite made me forget she had lost a son; to me, she was merely a wicked old witch who rejoiced in the sufferings of others.

In the meantime, one of the villagers saw me coming

down from Dead Man's Crag, which unleashed a veritable scandal at home.

In general Mother was right when she asked me, amid much shouting, what on earth I was doing on the crag, as if there weren't any other interesting places in the district, and why I absolutely had to climb a mountain which nobody else climbed. Of course, I said to myself, if Dead Man's Crag were just an ordinary mountain, what possible interest would there be in climbing it? That would truly have been stupid.

But I was unable to explain or to say anything in my own defence. Worse still, I could not even promise my mother never to go back to the crag, which was what annoyed her most, and she raised her arms to heaven in despair.

Finally, my father threatened me: 'If you climb up there again, I'll whip you!'

Father never made empty promises.

My obstinate silence was interpreted as heralding the arrival of the 'awkward age', and it was declared that my character was going to rack and ruin. This was certainly not the case, and I only hoped that once everything had been sorted out (if that ever happened), my parents would understand and forgive me.

Every morning I set off ostensibly for the shore and even used to give my parents the opportunity to check that I was nearby. But after an hour or two I would slip into the drop, sometimes lying low behind houses, sometimes behind fences, before starting the ascent of Dead Man's Crag. On one occasion my mother didn't find me by the lake and that evening she put me through a detailed interrogation about my timetable for the whole day; this was such torture that the next day I set off with my school book, announcing that I was going to prepare for next term and that it was boring to work indoors. I couldn't be obliged to read a textbook at the lakeside, at any rate in the middle of a crowd of boys; it was, I argued, quieter among the bushes or on the mountainside. In any case, Mother was touched by my zeal and, though somewhat surprised, I was granted permission to escape the constant supervision of my family.

Mothers are always eager to believe in the laudable intentions of their children. It would have taken a real swot to read a textbook in Baikal on a beautiful summer's day, instead of swimming and running in the hills.

And so it was, with my book slipped inside my shirt, that I appeared one day in the castle on Dead Man's Crag. In the course of the summer I had thoroughly forgotten my grammar and arithmetic, and when Ri asked me to tell her what was in my book I was greatly embarrassed. Gradually I took to swotting up my textbooks at home in the evenings, and telling Ri the next day about what I had read, which essentially took her mind off more painful matters, or at least so it seemed.

As for Mama, who would see me leaving home with a book, or indeed with two, and spending my evenings solving problems and swotting up grammatical rules when it was still daylight and I could perfectly well have been out in the fresh air – she, after observing my behaviour, regarded me with growing anxiety and held more and more muttered conferences with Father.

It was plain that only someone who was not quite normal could behave like this. Moreover, I regularly skipped lunch and was seldom out in the sun, since I was spending most of my time inside the castle; my face was therefore pale, or rather it wasn't suntanned like most of my other friends'.

A woman doctor was called to the house. She shrugged her shoulders and declared I ought to spend more time in the fresh air.

'But he spends all day outside!' exclaimed my mother despairingly.

The doctor listened to me again through her stethoscope from every angle and I felt quite sorry for her.

If Ri had gone to school, she would have obtained excellent marks all round. She grasped everything without the slightest difficulty, and after a few days the time came when I was literally unable to teach her anything new. After all, I couldn't study the syllabus of the class above mine. I wanted to read her my reading books, but my mother categorically forbade me to remove them from the house. So I used to spend my evenings reading and rereading the books in my possession, so as to tell Ri the stories the next day.

The fact that I had abandoned textbooks in favour of reading books was interpreted by my parents as a sign of recovery, though they would probably have been happy if I had thrown all my books and manuals under my bed.

One day (oh! how well I remember it!), Ri and I were chatting; I think I was telling her what our lessons were like at school, how we played at break time and in the evenings, and so on . . . That day, Ri was less animated than before, but at first I didn't notice. I told her that in a month's time it would be the beginning of term, and when I had said it, I realised with horror that then I would no longer be able to come to the crag. How was I going to survive? Feeling distraught, I stopped talking and Ri's face clouded over; within a second, it became as sad as it had been on my first visit.

As though guessing my thoughts, she said gently: 'And I will never . . . '

That was all she said. But the way she said it!

Baikolla looked at her anxiously. 'You mustn't.'

'I'm weary, Father!' said Ri, and just as she had done on my very first visit, she closed her eyes and laid her head on her father's hand.

'She's weary,' Baikolla echoed, and after a silence he added: 'You mustn't . . . you mustn't come again. She's weary.'

What sorrow and misery descended on me with those words! I stood beside Baikolla as though crushed to the ground by a gigantic rock, unable to move my limbs. Baikolla's head drooped on his chest and I could no longer see his eyes; I could only see his daughter's face, set in a mask of inhuman grief. Her eyes were open no more, and she might almost have been asleep, had it not been for the thin line on her forehead, signifying pain, the two darts of her eyebrows arched towards that line, her tightly clenched lips, harnessing tears of grief or humiliation, and her hair which fell as though in despair on to Baikolla's knees.

I stood there, not believing that this was the end. Tears began to flow from my eyes of their own accord; I couldn't check them. I didn't even try. I stumbled and fumbled my way up the castle steps, and when I emerged from the cave the sun did not dazzle me as it usually did, for I was seeing it through a veil of tears.

I walked a few steps from the cave and heard Sarma's grating voice: 'You've forgotten to close the entrance again, little scatterbrain.'

I dried my tears and looked at the old woman. Never until that moment had I felt such undiluted hatred for her. It actually made me tremble.

'Go and close it yourself if you feel like that about it!' I shouted, right in her face.

Sarma practically had a seizure.

'I'll . . . I'll . . . ' she stammered in absolute astonishment, but I didn't even let her finish the sentence. I leapt so close to her that she took a jump backwards and seemed to take root in the stony back of her throne.

'I'm not scared!' I shouted. 'You evil old woman, why are you torturing Ri?'

I went even closer. 'What's she done to you? What? You wicked thing! It's wickedness that's made you old, and your secrets haven't helped you in the slightest! You may know how to throw stones off the crag, but so do I!'

I picked up a stone from beneath her feet and, though heavy, I lifted it, walked towards the chasm and hurled it down; others followed suit, causing a creditable landslide, because, of course, when one stone crashes down the mountainside it dislodges others on the way.

I then shouted more abuse at the old woman, calling her terrible names. She had already got over her fear, or rather her amazement, and simply stared straight at me without blinking.

When I had shouted all I could, had yelled myself hoarse and practically choked, she said in a strange tone of voice: 'So you really want the little girl to live and be free?'

This put me on my guard, although I had not yet recovered from my fit of hysteria and my heart was beating so fast that I could hardly hear Sarma properly.

'Do you want to save her?' she asked again.

'Yes!' I cried, and the emotion that swept through me hit my head with a dull pain.

Sarma screwed up her eyes at me, looking suspicious or defiant (who could tell?), or possibly even scornful.

'Are you ready to perform a heroic deed to save her?'

Her voice now seemed to be sarcastic and I thought she was deceiving me, simply holding me up to ridicule, but none the less I said 'Yes!', although the expression 'heroic deed' struck me as altogether too bookish.

Sarma was silent, smacked her lips for a moment, then finally asked me in a solemn tone: 'Are you ready to do *anything* in order to save the daughter of Prince Baikolla?'

I could not really imagine what 'anything' might signify, but I certainly could give no answer other than 'yes'.

She fixed her eyes on me, as though she wanted them to pierce right through me. 'I'll give you a chance,' she said.

I did not immediately understand her meaning, but when I had grasped it, I froze into a state of feverish anticipation.

'Over there on that stone,' she said, pointing it out to me, 'there is a snake, a splendid specimen, long and fat. Go towards it, my fine friend, reach out and let it bite your hand. Afterwards, may your hand swell up like a boletus toadstool and may you know the pain and torture of snake poison. Go!'

Not yet believing her, I walked a short way, as though in a dream, towards the stone and there I really did see a huge fat adder, much bigger than the one Yurka had caught. I turned back to look at Sarma, hoping she had not been serious, that it had only been a joke, but from her expression I realised she was genuinely ordering me to do exactly as she had prescribed.

I shrank back from the snake which at that very moment moved all its coils, turned its head towards me and thrust out its forked tongue.

I jumped backwards, feeling my eyes hanging from my eyebrows with fear.

'I . . . I . . . ,' I stammered hoarsely, gulping back saliva.

I shook my head, waved my arms, my whole body racked by an utter inability to say: 'I won't!'

'Go and do as I tell you!' cried Sarma.

'No,' I yelped, in a loud, piercing voice.

'You're nothing but a shabby, rotten little field mushroom! So that's how much your goodness is worth! Not only my sons, but even the weakest, puniest child in the Valley of the Young Moon would have obeyed me without hesitation to save the daughter of Prince Baikolla. And that's not all. Anyone would have sacrificed his life! You're quivering and whining like a pup wihout a tail because you're afraid of a mere snakebite, which the most indolent healer would cure you of in two moons. You're just a pathetic pretence of a man. Get out of here! From now on, the path of suffering of the people of the valley is closed to you! Out of my sight! Go away! Go away! Go away!'

Sarma was trembling with rage. I didn't even notice how I had moved back to the start of the path down the crag; there was now nowhere left to move back to. I would have to go down. But just as I made to retreat, there rose before my eyes an image of the little girl in the castle, her brows drawn together with sadness. I can't remember exactly how it happened, but somehow, with my mouth open, my teeth chattering, my body trembling all over, I moved towards the stone where the snake was waiting for me. I was in a sort of trance, but I do recollect precisely the thoughts which flitted through my head in those moments: Vassina was down below, she would cure the snakebite, and if it hurt me, it wouldn't last all my life, and after a while it wouldn't hurt any more . . . a snake had bitten Yurka after all, and nothing had come of it . . . it was all over, and he was carrying on living as if nothing had happened . . .

The snake was staring at me, shooting out its tongue. But soon I no longer saw it; a veil of tears fell over everything and the fear which had knotted my body into a spasm began to emerge from my throat in a strange sound, halfway between, 'ah . . . ah . . . ah' and 'eh . . . eh . . . eh'. I began to scream in terror and another convulsion twisted my right hand which, in defiance of all fear, reached out of its own accord to the snake. I couldn't see it, but I was waiting for its bite like a flash of lightning or something still more terrifying; I couldn't pull my hand back, although it seemed as if I was putting all my strength into the attempt. My hand was still reaching towards the snake. I felt I was fainting.

Suddenly I heard Sarma's loud guffaw. I blinked several times to drive away the tears and when I opened my eyes I saw first my hand stretching ridiculously forward and then, a few inches from my fingers, the twisted, dried up, gnarled branch of a pine tree. *There was no snake!* I continued to hold out my hand, staring at it as if it didn't belong to me, and all the while Sarma laughed louder and louder, in ever more piercing tones. Eventually the feeling returned to my hand, which I hugged against my stomach as if it really had been bitten.

Sarma was roaring with laughter and squawking something or other through her mirth; I was meanwhile trying to grasp how this could have happened, how I had been able to hold out my own hand to the snake, even if it had turned out to be nothing but an ordinary lump of wood . . .

In later years I was to recall this scene many times, and

each time I was amazed; I would tell myself that when fear is so intense as to leave no room in the mind for anything but itself, it can be transformed into its opposite, and the act it dictates can seem like a heroic deed. It is curious to observe the large number of historical events which go under the name of heroic deeds which were actually performed in a state of pure terror.

As an adult, I find it very hard to envisage a situation in which I would voluntarily hold out my hand for a snake to bite. I dare to hope that life will never provide another opportunity as ridiculous and unpleasant as that one. But at the same time, I could not seriously claim to have been more daring as a child than I am now.

Be that as it may, the situation was this: Sarma was laughing uproariously, and I was standing in front of the stone, hugging my arm to my stomach.

'Come here!' commanded the old woman.

I went, simply obeying the order. I stopped near her, and felt sickness rising in my throat.

'Well?' she asked mockingly. 'Hasn't your little heart been torn into bits? Are you sagging at the knees?'

I didn't answer. Her mockery left me cold.

'Go home!' Sarma commanded. 'Consider that today, for the first time, you have lived a day of true life. That's enough for one day!'

These words were said in a voice I did not know, but I hadn't the strength to be glad about it.

'Off you go!' repeated Sarma. 'I'll close the entrance to the castle myself.'

The meaning of the words didn't filter through to me; I was even too tired to wonder: what entrance? to what castle? I turned round, sat on the usual ledge and slid down from it, but from then on I didn't exactly descend from the crag, but allowed myself to slip and slide all the way to the bottom. I dragged myself slowly along the path that led to the village, but before reaching it, I turned off into the bushes and lay down in the grass, where I remained until the cool of the evening.

Once I was in bed, Mother felt my forehead several times, put the thermometer in my mouth, examined it and shook it for a long time, looking at me anxiously all the while.

The following morning my parents talked with each other in the kitchen about how I had had another disturbed night and had been shouting about something to do with snakes, but hearing them mention snakes didn't alarm or upset me unduly. I felt sluggish and lay in bed for a long time. After lunch I went to Baikal and played with my friends, and life resumed its normal course. And every time I thought about Dead Man's Crag, I dismissed it from my mind straight away.

The same happened the next day, the whole of which I spent swimming with the other boys. I was almost used to the water temperature by then, although perhaps I would run to the wood fire on the shore more often than the others did.

After a few more days, I overheard another conversation between my parents; they were saying that the night when I had shouted and talked about snakes had been 'critical' for me, but that now I was looking better, and recovering. Mother and Father were pleased, although I, for my part, had completely forgotten where I had put my textbooks and reading books.

5

YURKA AND I were repairing the raft. During the night there had been a strong north-easterly wind – the Barguzin again – which had thrown our raft on to a rock and two of the logs had cracked where they were fastened together. First of all we levered out the clamps using whatever came to hand, then hammered them into new places, and finally bound the split logs with wire. We were still trying to haul the raft off the rock and into the water when Valerka ran up and told us that White Grandad – Genka the boatman's grandfather – was dying. The doctor from Slyudyanka had been called out and was coming over on the railwayman's trolley.

We raced along the shore to Genka's house where many people had already gathered. Genka himself, lips swollen and eyes red, was sitting on the edge of a boat on the shore, looking confused.

'Is he still alive?' asked Yurka.

Genka sniffed and his eyes flashed. 'He's not going to die! That woman doctor of ours doesn't understand a thing. The doctor from Slyudyanka will tell us the true story when he gets here!'

'Maybe we should call old Vassina – she's a witch after all . . . she can . . . '

Genka shook his head. 'No, she won't come.'

'Why not?' I asked.

'She just won't,' said Genka with conviction. 'She has hated Grandad all her life.'

'Nonsense,' Yurka scowled. 'She helps everybody.'

'Everybody else. But she hates Grandad.'

'What for? What's he done to her?'

'He's done nothing. She hates him, and that's all there is to it.'

Genka's mother appeared in the porch of the house. She sat down on the step, buried her face in her hands and seemed to be crying. Genka started sniffling even more loudly.

Another woman emerged from the house and said gloomily: 'What a state of affairs! He's asking for old Vassina to come!'

Quite right, I thought. The old man knows who can help him.

Genka's mother shook her head. 'She won't come.'

'I know she won't,' the other woman agreed.

'But he's dying! How can she *not* come? She must!'

I could not understand such a thing and since I knew where she lived I was contemplating going to get her myself, when suddenly I heard a whisper of amazement: 'There she is! You see, she *is* a witch! It's as if she heard!'

I almost jumped for joy. I had known she would come. I had liked her from the start, the old dear. Even if she hadn't allowed Yurka to kill the snake!

Everyone greeted her and made way for her to enter. Genka's mother followed. No one said a word. I was so curious to know how she would treat the old man that I longed to rush through the door after her. But, of course, no one would have let me. I dashed about, running round the outside of the house looking first in one window, then in another, until I saw White Grandad. He was lying on a bed or, rather, half sitting with his elbows propped up on some large pillows. His face was a sort of greyish-green colour, his breathing laboured, and his left hand gripped the edge of the sheet.

I saw Vassina go into the room with Genka's mother, who left again immediately. Standing on tiptoe and clinging to the wooden shutter, I pressed my nose and one eye against the window and held my breath.

'You've come, Anyuta!' Grandad croaked, and I thought for a moment his mind was wandering, but then realised that Anyuta was in fact the old woman's name. How strange, she was always known simply as 'old Vassina' and probably nobody knew her real name or else everybody had forgotten it.

'Yes, I have,' she replied quietly, and sat down on a chair beside the old man's bed. She had nothing in her hands and I couldn't imagine how she intended to cure him.

'I'm dying, you know,' said Grandad.

'You are indeed,' Vassina agreed, and a shiver ran through my bones.

They looked at each other.

'Do you repent, Grisha?' she asked.

'I do, I do . . . ' Grandad answered hurriedly.

'Why didn't you before?'

'I did . . . I've always repented . . . But I knew you wouldn't forgive me!'

The old woman nodded, perhaps in agreement, perhaps involuntarily.

'Give me some water! My throat's dry – I can't speak.'

Vassina handed him a glass from the stool by the bed. He tried to take it in his hand, but could not, so she helped him, drying his lips afterwards with a towel which was hanging on the back of the bed.

'You didn't leave the grave, did you? Were you afraid?'

'I did leave it, Anyuta – with a cross, as one should.'

'You left it!' Vassina groaned. 'So there is a grave!'

She closed her eyes and shook her head. 'And how am I to forgive you for such a thing, Grisha? How?'

'Forgive me as you see fit,' said Grandad in a hoarse whisper.

'Where is it? Tell me!'

'I'll tell you where it is,' replied the old man, starting to cough and tremble. 'You'll find it, don't worry. There is a little spring in the Dry Gully, you know it . . . well, above the spring . . . you'll see a notch cut in a pine tree . . . It wasn't for profit, Anyuta! People were talking . . . about gold . . . There wasn't any gold there . . . never had been . . . It was because of a quarrel . . . it was stupid . . . '

I had great difficulty in keeping my balance on the mound of earth below the window and the strain involved prevented me from fully understanding what they were saying.

Grandad wanted to add something but he was once again overcome by a coughing fit and Vassina told him to stay silent. The old man's white beard leapt up and down on his chest as he coughed.

The earth beneath me began to move. I lost my foothold and fell to the ground. Scrambling to my feet, I tore away from the house towards the other boys and, as a precaution, hid among them. They asked me some questions and I gave some replies, trying all the while to piece together and make sense of the snatches of conversation I had heard.

'Vassina's come out!' cried Yurka, and Genka leapt up and ran into the house.

The old woman had almost gone past us when she stopped, turned towards us, and beckoned with her finger – to me, of course. Red as a lobster, I went over to her.

She looked at me calmly, stroked my head and said: 'There are some things in life that it profits no one to know!'

What a voice she had! I took her hand in both of mine, squeezed it tight, and whispered fervently, 'May my parents die should I tell a soul!'

But Vassina shook her head. 'Even if you tell the whole world, may your parents live. There can be no secrets worth more than your own mother and father!'

I immediately felt ashamed of my foolish oath. She stroked my head once more and went on her way. I was besieged by the other boys, eager to discover what we had been talking about. I told some fib.

White Grandad was taken away on the rail-trolley to Slyudyanka. Genka went with him, shouting to us as they left that he would bring his grandfather back in good health.

I spent a long time walking on the shores of Lake Baikal thinking about what I had heard. And although I thought I knew what had taken place in the forest at Dry Gully and perceived it to be frightening and fascinating, there was one phrase which for some reason kept coming back to me. I even said it out loud in an attempt to recreate Vassina's own intonation: 'And how am I to forgive you for such a thing, Grisha?'

When at last I succeeded in reproducing the intonation precisely, joyful suspicion turned into certainty. For I realised that with those words old Vassina had already forgiven White Grandad! And when he replied, 'Forgive as you see fit,' it was as much as to say: 'Thank you!'

When I thought of the other old woman who could not and would not forgive, then I remembered everything else besides – not that I had really ever forgotten, only I had vowed to myself not to think about it.

And what about the business with the snake? Was it just another of Sarma's jokes? But what if it was not? What if she was serious in her promise to free Ri? How many days I had lost! How could I have forgotten and thought about anything except what was most important!

I would run immediately to Sarma and demand that she fulfil her promise. And even if the snake turned out to be no more than a stick, that stick nevertheless *had been* a snake and I had stretched out my hand to it! I had stretched out my hand!

Never before had I climbed Dead Man's Crag so quickly – all in one breath, it seemed. I appeared before Sarma, breathless, but full of resolution.

'But she's gone already!' said Sarma with a wily grin.

'Gone! Where?'

'She's living among people. Aren't you pleased?'

I was confused and hurriedly tried to sort out my own feelings. I had not foreseen this turn of events.

'But where is she?' I asked again.

'I've told you, she is living among people!'

'But I . . . ' I was at a loss for words.

'You should be glad, but I see no sign of it,' said Sarma spitefully. 'You were hoping, of course, that I would simply deliver her into your hands so you could take her away and marry her!'

There was no question – the old woman had taken leave of her senses. In one respect, however, she was right. A thousand times I had imagined myself leading Ri out of the cave into the sun, taking her to the village and showing her Lake Baikal.

'May I see her?'

'What for? She doesn't know you now.'

'She doesn't know me!' I cried in horror.

Sarma smiled mockingly, but spoke without malice: 'How could she live among people if she remembered everything? Do you really believe she could?'

'But . . . has she forgotten everything? Her father, the legend . . . everything?' I wanted to say 'even me', but held back.

'Of course,' replied Sarma. 'Otherwise she could not live.'

It was an unthinkable, cruel truth. Impossible to object, but even harder to agree.

'But what about Baikolla? Is he . . . alone . . . all alone now?'

Sarma frowned angrily.

'Silence! Don't dare to say any more! What I have done is more than you could begin to comprehend. But I still have not told you everything. Are you capable of listening and understanding?'

'Yes.'

I lied. I was not capable of understanding anything at all. My thoughts, like drunkards, reeled in my head, crashing into each other.

Sarma spoke in a solemn, moralising tone. 'I have freed Baikolla's little girl! That means I have freed her from sorrow. That is the essential thing. You, too, could have taken her out of the castle, but could you have given her peace of mind? That's the point! But can you understand that sadness and sorrow do not exist without Man, that to free one person from sorrow means to give it to someone else? Can you understand that?'

I nodded, but of course it was a lie. I did not understand.

'Hear this, then! *You* have taken her sorrow upon yourself. The time will come when you, the sickly child of unhappy parents, will cry out from the burden of the load you have taken on, and you will come running to me, begging me to free you, and I shall free you, I promise, for such a burden is too great for your puny shoulders. And then the girl will return, for the place of sadness cannot remain empty. Guilt, which gives rise to sadness, never disappears, so sadness and sorrow are eternal. The girl will return to her father, and you will forget all you knew. That is how it will be.'

'She will not return!' I cried. 'And that is not how it will be!'

From all that Sarma had said I understood that through my fault Ri could end up captive in the crag again. But if it depended on me, that would never happen! At that moment I felt that I would stretch my hand out to the snake a hundred times if necessary. Or do something even more terrible . . .

Sarma smiled disdainfully and pulled a face.

'May I go and see him?'

'Go and ask if he is pleased.'

When I approached Baikolla he was the first to speak – which had not happened before – and in a voice which I had not yet heard: 'You know already! She is living among people. Tell Sarma I am grateful to her!'

'But you . . . how will you . . . . ?'

His white eyebrows dropped, and the light in his eyes faded, but they were different eyes now, quite different, and only at that point did I realise that Ri had taken a share of his sadness away from here.

'Me – that's another matter,' he said serenely. 'But she had not lived . . . Have you seen her then?'

'No,' I replied bitterly. But that I would never see her, I did not say.

'If you see her you will be kind to her, won't you? You are a good son, of good parents, and I believe that on the night of your maturity, the stars will give you a worthy name!'

I realised then why they had never asked my name – they thought I did not yet have one! And Sarma had not asked either, though of course my name would have been of no use to her.

Baikolla bent down from his chair and stroked the puppy. Now that Ri was no longer in the castle, it stared at her chair with eyes so unhappy that one could not look into them without feeling pain.

Baikolla said to me: 'Take him with you! And may he become your friend!'

I protested. How could I leave Baikolla all alone without the dog which was at least another living being to have near?

'Take him! He too has not yet lived!'

I took the young dog in my arms; he nestled up to me and for some reason began to shake.

'May I come and visit you?'

At first Baikolla shook his head as if to say 'What's the point?' But then he said: 'Should you meet my daughter among the people, come and tell me about her.'

'I shall come without fail.'

But deep inside my heart ached at the thought that, perhaps, I would never see either Ri or Baikolla again.

I said goodbye and turned to leave. The strange thing was that as I went up the steps and through the halls and the cave to the exit, the creature in my arms grew heavier and heavier. By the time the midday sun pierced my eyes, the animal which jumped down from my arms was no longer a puppy but an almost fully grown dog so that when it stood up on its hind legs, its front paws touched my shoulders.

Sarma saw the dog and pulled a long face. But I forestalled her: 'Baikolla gave me him as a present.'

She muttered something under her breath but said nothing aloud, which meant she granted permission.

'I'll call him Friend. Baikolla said he should become my friend, so that's what I shall call him!'

Sarma did not deign to look at me. I went up and sat beside her, and Friend sat next to me.

'Tell me,' I ventured, 'will you really never forgive Baikolla?'

She hissed angrily through her teeth: 'I'm too lenient with you, and it does no good!'

'But I know another woman, and she forgave the man who killed her own . . . ' (I did not know exactly whom.)

Sarma looked at me with pity.

'You're not a very good liar, are you? You think up some fairy-tale and imagine that I won't be able to tell it from the truth! But you do that only because you can't understand that forgiveness is impossible. If a crime has been committed, and if there is sorrow in the soul, then there can be no forgiveness. I've explained this to you already. To forgive is to betray sorrow, to forget it. Weak people who forget their sorrow and in their weakness renounce vengeance, give the name "forgiveness" to their weakness and failure to remember. And again, if the person who is forgiven is guilty, do you think he will forget his guilt just because someone says: "I forgive you"? The guilty do not need forgiveness, because they know they cannot escape their own guilt. And if the woman you mentioned really existed and if she did say, "I forgive you", then she was either lying, or else she had already forgotten the person she had lost. Forgiveness! Just think about it! It's like saying guilt is not guilt, and sorrow is not sorrow. It's even quite laughable!'

She spoke to me with condescension, but I felt just as condescending towards her, because I had heard the words of forgiveness with my own ears, at the window of Genka's house, and with my own eyes I had seen the sorrow on the face of the woman who spoke them. Yet to understand that was not within Sarma's power. And for the first time it occurred to me that quite possibly she was really rather stupid, or at least not very clever, which made her even more unhappy – unhappier than old Vassina. Unhappy because she was incapable of forgiving. I began to feel sorry for Sarma, and even sorrier for Baikolla, and from all these feelings and doubts a quiet pain entered my heart.

I was quite unable to conceive of the fact that Prince Baikolla's daughter was living somewhere among ordinary people, knowing nothing of herself and remembering nothing . . .

'So I shall never see Ri again?'

'Perhaps you will. Perhaps you won't,' replied Sarma.

'Perhaps I will?'

She shrugged her shoulders inconclusively, giving nothing away. 'But if you do see her, remember this: if you so much as hint at what she has forgotten, and must not remember, you will cause her pain. She won't remember in any case, but she will suffer all the same.'

I did not pay much attention to these words, but they did light a tiny spark of hope in my heart.

'Well, let's be going,' I said, stroking Friend.

Sarma looked at me and made an ambiguous gesture with her hand, as though she wished to add something but found it difficult to express.

'There is no need for me to tell you this, but I suppose I shall . . . No one summoned you here, but from the moment you arrived . . . and meddled in things . . . ' She shook her head, surprised by her own words. 'You're just a young chicken, despite your strong spirit, and yet you come meddling . . . '

It seemed as though she herself did not understand how it was that I had 'come meddling'.

'You now share a great secret,' she continued, 'and that is no reason to rejoice, as you will soon understand. So let this be your reward: know that as long as you live on these shores, nothing bad will happen to you.'

'But what could happen to me?' I asked, bewildered.

'A great deal could happen to such a puny little flower!' Sarma replied mockingly.

Tired of her taunting, I could no longer make the effort to understand the meaning of her words. I took my leave of her as politely as possible and set off down the crag with my dog. Friend leapt from stone to stone and from ledge to ledge as though he did it every day and I soon stopped telling him the way and warning him of the dangers of slipping. Now I merely praised him, and to every word of praise or attention he replied with his tail, his eyes and his ears, apparently understanding everything.

At home I announced to my parents, in plain terms that pre-empted any objections, that the dog was a gift and would be living with us. My father and mother exchanged perplexed looks and my mother said: 'Well, we don't really mind, do we?'

'Let him stay!' said Father. 'But we'll have to find a place for him.'

So Father spent the rest of the day building a kennel for Friend beside the porch. I refused point-blank to have him put on a chain and Father, placatory, said, 'We'll see.' But when I declared that if they chained Friend up, they could chain me up too, Father became uneasy and started trying to persuade Mother that such a clever dog would never dream of slaying the hens or biting good people. For these just words, Friend thanked my father with a wag of his tail.

In the evening Svetka's father came and said that White Grandad had died in the hospital at Slyudyanka. I felt very sorry both for the old man and for Genka.

'What can be done!' said Mother.

'The doctor predicted that Grandad would suffer terribly before his death; that's the kind of illness it was. But when he died it was as though he was leaving for a different world.'

My father spread his hands and said: 'No matter what anyone says, medicine only goes skin-deep. Yes . . . And when Grandad died, the story of our local gold died too.'

'There wasn't a speck of gold there!' I shouted from the kitchen.

They all came into the kitchen, and Father asked: 'There wasn't a speck of gold where?'

'In Dry Gully.'

'In Dry Gully?' Svetka's father exclaimed. 'That's right, there is a gully by that name. But how do you know about it?'

I regretted saying what I had even though I had not blurted out anything terribly important. I remembered Vassina's words about secrets which it profited nobody to know.

'I just happen to know!' I replied, making it clear that they would not succeed in drawing another word out of me.

'Well, well,' said Svetka's father in surprise. 'So there's a rumour about Dry Gully too. I've lived here all my days and never heard that one. I don't believe there's any gold around here either. Geologists went over the whole area long ago and found lots of things, but no gold. Dry Gully, eh? There's a thing! White Grandad used to have a winter cabin there, then there was a fire and for some reason the wild animals started to keep away from that gully. There's no water there, of course, only a tiny spring for miles around.'

Meanwhile the nut-gathering season came round and one by one the boys began to disappear for several days at a time from the banks of Lake Baikal. They would reappear with black resin marks on their hands, cheeks, brows and necks, and although resin is easily enough removed with kerosene or petrol, the boys seemed in no hurry to get rid of the stains. Their pockets were now full of nuts, and conversations round the camp fires on the beach centred exclusively on nut-gathering. One boasted that when he struck a cedar tree with his beater, a single blow brought down two hundred cones, ten of which hit him on the head. Gradually the number of cones falling at one blow rose to five hundred, and the boys would jealously examine the backs of each other's necks for signs of direct hits.

One boy's beater had broken from the force of his strike, another's hut had caught fire during the night, a third had had all his food and provisions dragged off by a wolverine at night and yet another had discovered fresh bear prints near his cabin.

I was the only one to sit listening and eating. They all fed me with nuts and demanded to know whose were roasted best. I did not even know how to crack them properly. The other boys just bit through the shells and in the time it took me to struggle through ten, they had polished off a whole handful.

But at last the morning came when I too, haversack on my back, marched along the narrow forest path that led to the cedar woods. Ahead of me walked Svetka's father – or Uncle Seryozha as I called him – then Yurka and his brother Vitya. Svetka followed, hard on my heels.

The path twisted and turned, rose and fell, and even disappeared completely in places. We had been walking for more than an hour, but I didn't feel tired – only glad, for it had not been easy to persuade Mother to let me go and she probably would not have granted permission had Uncle Seryozha not been escorting us. What nonsense Mother spoke in her attempt to foil my plans: that I was too weak and would not survive the long walk; that I might get cold at night (for we were to sleep out in the open); that I had not recovered from my illness; and a great deal more besides – all unfair and unnecessary. Be that as it may, I was now walking along the path and had already gone too far for anybody to try to send me back.

We had set out before dawn, hardly able to see the way at first, and the cold early-morning breeze from Baikal switched our backs. Then it grew light, the sun rose behind us and the chirping of birds rang in my unaccustomed ears. But as we went further, the forest grew gloomier and it became much quieter. We were already surrounded by cedars with cones hanging from their branches and on their crowns, and I could not understand why we were marching straight past them, or why we had to go so far when we could collect as many cones as we wanted there. I asked Svetka, who scoffed: 'Call these cedars! There's only a dozen cones on each of them! It would take you a week to gather enough!'

Along the way we passed many interesting things, wondrous and unfamiliar, but we were here 'on business' and there was no time to stand and gaze. The huge ant-hills and the fallen cedars with their roots torn out of the ground made a particularly strong impression.

Many times the path divided, and at one such fork Uncle Seryozha shouted at me: 'Do you see?' and pointed to a path leading off to the left.

We arrived at a large shelter put together with branches and poles. We quickly drank some tea and then set to work, splitting into two groups. Yurka and his brother went one way, while Svetka, her father and I went another. To make our 'beater' Uncle Seryozha chopped down a large birch tree, sawed off a section about a metre long, cut a slanting groove in the middle of it, and hammered a long rod into the groove. It was so heavy I could hardly lift it.

Svetka and I took a bag each, and Uncle Seryozha placed the beater with its shaft on the ground in front of the first cedar. He pulled the beater back, then hurled it against the tree-trunk. The cones teemed down, some whistling past and sinking into the moss, others rustling and bounding through the branches, ricocheting off the trunk in all directions.

'Get gathering!' shouted Svetka.

I dived up to the tree and, rummaging about on the ground, managed to find five cones. Uncle Seryozha struck the tree again and something hit me so hard on the back that I fell down in the moss with a cry. Svetka rolled about with laughter. When I got up I saw she already had about fifty cones in her bag. It was such hard work. Uncle Seryozha kept on beating, and I rushed about under the trees, trampling into the moss more cones than I gathered. Svetka, in contrast, feared nothing; she started picking up the cones as they were still falling from the tree. They struck her on the head and shoulders, and she squealed and shrieked and laughed, and I could not understand how she was not hurt. After only three hits, my head was buzzing, my arm ached so much I could not bear to touch it, and my spine felt as if it had been cracked in two. My feet, like my back, were tired and aching, and were for ever sinking into the moss and slipping on the stones.

We put all our cones together in heaps, and as we moved about from one part of the forest to another, I wondered how we would ever find them all again.

Just as I was beginning to feel that I could not go a single step further, Uncle Seryozha suggested that Svetka and I should go to the shelter and prepare lunch. Svetka shouted, 'Let's go!' but I had not the faintest idea of which direction to take. Svetka showed me the way as if she were walking through the village; it turned out to be very close because we had simply been moving in circles round the shelter. While we prepared lunch, Uncle Seryozha and Vitya began bringing the cones to the shelter by the sackful.

I ate Svetka's soup as I had never eaten my mother's – I just could not have enough of it. Then I lay down on my back and fell asleep at once. When they woke me, we went off to work again, and strangely enough, it was all much easier after lunch. I had the knack now of noticing where the cones dropped and finding them quickly, and I had learned more or less how to dodge them when they fell, although even Svetka could not avoid them altogether.

Towards evening we were again sent off to prepare some food. Then we cut down some dead trees and dragged them to the shelter: we needed a fire for the whole evening which was to be spent processing the cones. Next, we got a large tarpaulin from the shelter and spread it on the ground, and also brought out sieves with holes of various sizes. Then we lit the fire.

Earlier I had noticed a large wooden block with little teeth notched out of it. It was on this that each cone was placed, then rubbed in a single sweep with a little board which also had teeth. The whole mountain of cones had to be processed in this way. Then the nuts obtained by this method had to be sieved three times and finally roasted on a griddle over the fire.

Yurka and the men rubbed the cones, and Svetka and I put the nuts through the sieves. So engrossed was I in this work that I did not even notice night falling. The mountain of cones seemed to grow no smaller. But when it did at last diminish, Yurka came over to help with the sieving, and I was able to relax a little. The first lot of nuts was already over the fire, and I was entrusted with the task of stirring them round so that they would not burn. Some of them did burn, however, and the scorched shells burst open and shot straight into my face.

'Well, now you know how nuts are gathered!' said Uncle Seryozha. 'You won't want to come again!'

'I will!' I replied, though rather unsurely.

Everything comes to an end, and so, too, did our work. The cleaned and roasted nuts were poured into our haversacks. I was given four potfuls on the assumption I could not carry more. Svetka also got four, but Yurka got six, which was humiliating: I was no weaker than he was, and why should I be compared with Svetka! But I did not argue. Uncle Seryozha's and Vitya's sacks were so heavy that it was hard to believe that anyone could even lift them from the ground.

'Now let's have a good long sleep!' said Uncle Seryozha.

In the shelter we found blankets, old but with no holes in them, quilted jackets, and even fur hats. I already knew that nights in the Baikal forests could be very cold.

The men settled themselves at the fire, and we three children were assigned to the shelter. Yurka went there straight away, but Svetka and I asked to sit awhile at the fire.

The night was very dark. Only now, as I looked around me, did I sense how frightening it all was. The light from the fire extended only a couple of paces and, beyond that, the forest clearing was full of terrifying shadows, rustlings, and all sorts of unfamiliar and worrying noises. Against the sky I could see the vague outline of the cedar trees, and it seemed as if their tops were hanging over our heads, ready to bear down on us at any moment, like living monsters of the night. I thought I could hear movements in the darkness, as though somebody was creeping up or walking nearby, and I wanted to move in as close as possible to the fire for safety.

'Are you scared?' whispered Svetka.

I gave a snort as if I could not care less.

'I always feel scared at night!' confessed Svetka, so I agreed that it was not very pleasant.

Everyone else was asleep by now, but we still sat listening to the sounds of the night and gazing into the fire. I was rather apprehensive about going off to the dark shelter, so I announced I was going to stay there. Wrapping a quilted jacket round me, I lay down beside the big block with the teeth cut out of it and soon fell asleep.

When I awoke, it was hot and sunny and already past noon. Lunch – or breakfast – was ready. My whole body ached as if I had been kicked and beaten with sticks. But Svetka pulled me off to a stream and made me have a long wash, after which I felt lighter and fresher, and Yurka and I even wrestled for a while in the glade.

We placed large cones in the corners of our haversacks, tied broad, soft straps to the sides, and fastened them at the tops. The men helped Svetka, Yurka and me to put on ours before putting on their own; this they did by sitting down at first, then rising with difficulty, swaying a little, then grunting approvingly. My own sack seemed light, and I was ashamed to be carrying only as much as a girl.

We walked back in the same order as we had come. We had not covered a kilometre before I started to feel the straps on my shoulders, and soon I no longer regretted carrying only four potfuls. I tried putting my palms under the straps, and already walked with my back bent instead of straight. It was no fun at all now . . .

But something happened at the halfway mark on our return journey. At the same fork in the path where the day before Uncle Seryozha had shouted something to us (we'd since forgotten what), old Vassina suddenly appeared in front of us. My companions were no less surprised than I was. She wore a thick jacket and boots, and carried a stick in her hand.

'How do you come to be walking all alone in the forest, Vassina?' asked Uncle Seryozha. 'You could run into wild animals, you know! You're on your way back from Dry

Gully, are you?' (That's what I'd wanted to say to Svetka's father the previous evening: that the path led to Dry Gully.)

'The place where I have been, Seryozha, is the place I'm returning from,' she replied with a smile.

'So you *were* there,' said Uncle Seryozha, looking fixedly at old Vassina. 'If only you'd told me, I would have gone with you. It doesn't do for someone of your advanced years to be roaming the forest alone.'

Vassina said nothing; she merely smiled and narrowed her eyes at us. We took our leave, and everyone, except me, proceeded along the path. Letting Svetka go in front of me, I stopped for a minute, went up to the old woman, and asked in a whisper: 'Did you . . . did you find it? Yes?'

Just as before, she stroked my head. Mother also liked to slide her fingers through my hair, though I myself hated it. But with the old woman, it was quite a different sensation. For with her, I wanted her stroking to go on and on. She had such an extraordinary touch.

'I found it. I found it,' she replied. 'For forty years I searched, and now I have found it.'

'Forty years!' I exclaimed.

'And now I am ready for the longest road of all . . . ' she said, as if to herself. 'But go now! Go! You're falling behind and it's easier if you walk with the others.'

'Goodbye!'

She inclined her head.

As I walked, I thought to myself who is it she has down there in Dry Gully? Her son? Her husband?

I tried to imagine a murder scene, but couldn't work out White Grandad's part in it. The picture just did not fit. Could we take her in to live with us, I wondered. But then, would she agree? Forty years of living on her own – it was unthinkable! Sarma, of course, had already sat alone for goodness knows how many years on Dead Man's Crag. No one could make an exact count, because people didn't even know that Lake Baikal had taken the place of the Valley of the Young Moon.

I caught up with Svetka but the others were still out of sight. We trailed by more than a kilometre. Already I felt barely able to crawl and had to rest every fifty paces or so.

When I arrived home, Father took the haversack from my back, and my body felt so light when relieved of its burden that I staggered around uncontrollably. Mother fumed when she saw the resin marks covering my face, hair and hands, but nothing could force me to remove these traces which had been acquired through such hard work. The following day I would meet my friends on the beach – this time on equal terms – with my own nuts in my pocket and with something that I, too, could boast about. I could feel two quite definite lumps on the back of my head, and my only fear was that they might disappear in the course of the night.

I finished supper and went to bed. Falling asleep was like a leap into nothingness.

The month of August drew to a close, and the aspen wood, burnt by the sun, appeared as ribbons of yellow on the slopes. The green of the birch trees was also fading and it was as if nature were preparing itself for a change of clothes. Evenings became colder, but the days were still quite warm, and although one wasn't really meant to bathe after St Ilya's Day (long since past) we would still play in the water till we turned blue.

I often used to go to the beach with Friend. He swam

better than I, even though I also did a kind of doggy-paddle. He would fetch pieces of wood which I threw into the lake for him, and would sit faithfully by my clothes when I played in the water with the other boys.

In general, he was such an intelligent dog that everyone was quite surprised by him. Everyone, that is, except me, for I alone knew where he had come from. He never bit anyone, though he refused to admit strangers. If he was teased, then he bore it patiently; if threatened, he simply showed his teeth in silence. The other village dogs bristled when they saw him and always gave him a wide berth.

Friend had only one little shortcoming: he simply never barked. He understood and obeyed all my commands, but when I told him to bark, he just wagged his tail. And there was something else. Although he would play with me quite cheerfully, and run and jump, his eyes would always remain sad, and my heart felt heavy just to look at them.

I did not go to Dead Man's Crag any more, though that didn't mean I had forgotten about it. Far from it. In fact, each time I looked into Friend's eyes, I thought I detected a kind of silent reproach, as if he were saying to me: 'How do you expect me to be happy and play around and enjoy myself when UP THERE . . . '

Friend and I sometimes went into the drop where we would sit for a long time on the stones at the foot of Dead Man's Crag. But most often we would climb on to the cliff over the nearest railway tunnel. On the Baikal side, it was practically perpendicular. We would sit on the top and gaze at the lake. And sometimes I would proclaim the legend with Friend listening attentively and looking sadly into the horizon above the lake. If ever I forgot something and faltered over a word, he would look at me as if he wanted to prompt, and when I remembered and continued the story, he would wag his tail gently and turn again to the dark-blue skyline.

'The mighty Sibir bent down and tore out the icy mountain range by the roots. He raised it high above his head . . . ' With this I would pick up a large stone and lift it up over my head. ' . . . he looked to the north, then to the south . . . ' I turned to the left, then to the right, with Friend doing likewise. ' . . . then looked to the east, then to the west. But there was nowhere to throw the mountain range, for there were living things all around. So he turned it above his head and threw it into the heavens . . . '

And with that, I would throw my stone skywards. Far from soaring into the sky, however, it would only travel a little way up before falling into the water, and when there were no waves I would watch it descending slowly into the dark-blue shadows of the deep.

But when Lake Baikal was stormy, we would simply sit on the cliff, gazing at the waves and listening to their rumble, in the knowledge that this was no ordinary rumble but one which told a story, the story of the death of the Valley of the Young Moon.

The first of September arrived – hardly a joyful occasion for me – and the morning found me in an unusually sad mood. It seemed to me that everything connected with Dead Man's Crag was being moved aside to make way for the school term, and that in turn left everything only half-clear, only half-complete. From now on, the days at school threatened to keep the secret of the crag from me.

My parents woke me in the morning, gave me breakfast, got all the necessary things together and, before leaving for school themselves, warned me not to be late for the ceremonial lining-up which takes place on the first day back.

I got ready quickly, hoping to arrive a little early so that I could make friends with the children who boarded. The upper storey of the school building was given over to boarders who came from remote little railway-halts along the line.

I took my schoolbag and went out on to the porch. Friend came out of his kennel and greeted me with his tail and eyes. Force of habit rather than any hope of success made me tell him to bark, and to my amazement he did! I couldn't believe my ears and repeated the command again and again, and each time Friend complied, his eyes full of joy. Valerka, who happened to be passing, was also astonished, and together the three of us played, jumped and barked until we quite forgot about school. When we did remember, we took to our heels. There was nothing worse than the children of teachers arriving late for the line-up!

But, of course, we were late. The ceremony was over and all the children were already going to their classrooms. Valerka scampered ahead and managed to find two places at the back. I ran hard on his heels but at the door of the classroom I stopped, rooted to the spot. I closed my eyes and opened them again, not believing what I saw.

At the first desk in the middle sat Prince Baikolla's daughter, young Ri of Dead Man's Crag. She was dressed in a brown school tunic with a light-blue ribbon in her hair. I rushed up to the desk and stood in front of her, my face breaking into a happy smile. She looked at me quite dispassionately, a little surprised perhaps, before turning away. But she had not recognised me! My happy smile became idiotic and with this silly expression I made my way through the rows, not seeing anything in front of me, and tripping over legs and desks, till I took my place next to Valerka, who had already been signalling to me for some time.

She's here! And my heart beat with joy. She doesn't know me. And my heart contracted into a lump which threatened to turn to stone.

The schoolmistress entered the classroom whereupon we all rose and sat down again. When the roll call started I listened out not only for my own name but also for the one I wanted to learn. When Ri got up to answer, the extra-ordinary voice that I knew so well (it had not changed) produced such a strange effect on me that my throat became quite dry.

Afterwards we were given our places. I hoped that I would not have to sit at the same desk as Ri and was relieved to be put next to Svetka, which was an exceptionally good seat, at the third desk in the left-hand row. From this position I was able to see Ri without her being able to notice my attentions.

Feigning nonchalance, I asked Svetka: 'Who is that girl?'

'That's Rimka. She's a boarder. She lives eighty kilometres from here.'

This new name saddened me. Though I knew it was the only first name that could be made from 'Ri', it neverthe-less seemed cold, somehow alien and inexpressive. If the astrologer had given her her real name, according to the custom of the Valley of the Young Moon, then surely that would have been beautiful.

In spite of everything, I couldn't quite believe that she remembered absolutely nothing. I thought of finding her during the first break and asking her if she remembered me and had quite resolved to do so, only in the event I thought better of it and did not ask her. I imagined I could hear Sarma telling me that such a question would cause her pain.

Though I asked her nothing, I took time to look into her eyes. True enough, they were not as sad as on the mountain, but one could not exactly say they were happy either. The pain was gone from her eyes, but the sadness remained and as I observed her during the break, she did not smile even once.

I spent the four lessons and three breaks as if in a day-dream. After the last bell I was the first to bolt from the classroom and, after hiding my bag in the bushes behind the school, I ran like the wind in the direction of the drop.

Sarma greeted me with a smile. 'You seem to be pleased!'

I answered her with a stupid grin.

'Silly little fool,' she said. 'You have your whole life ahead of you and you'll live to regret it.'

But I did not want to hear or listen to these bad words and, without asking permission, I threw myself towards the stone which blocked the entrance to the castle. I slid down the steps and, still a long way off, I called out to Baikolla across the hall: 'She's here, I mean she's with us!'

'You saw her! Is she well! Happy?' asked Baikolla, full of emotion.

I nodded, though the question concerning her happiness would need a little more reflection.

'And you won't cause her pain, you'll protect her from harm, won't you?'

I nodded again.

'She ought to be allowed to live. She hasn't until now. I'm at peace now. Don't let anyone hurt her!'

'No. No one.' Just let anyone try, I thought.

I went right up to Baikolla and touched his hands with

mine: 'Perhaps I could ask Sarma if she would do the same for you . . . '

He winced and interrupted: 'It's not worth it. Be my daughter's friend and the stars will grant you happiness!'

Be her friend . . . that I would gladly be. But she did not know me. I did not say this to Baikolla – besides, I could be her friend secretly without her being obliged to know about it.

The main thing was that she was now in the village, which meant I could see her every day. Indeed, during those first days it really did seem that this was the essential thing and that I was more than happy simply to be able to see her and protect her.

Shortly afterwards, however, after about a week perhaps, the tiny worm of sorrow began to gnaw at my happiness. I don't know why, but after getting to know all my class-mates, I was still unable to speak to Baikolla's daughter, simply incapable of engaging her on any subject what-soever. We behaved towards the other girls without ceremony, without picking our words particularly. But I could not, for example, bring myself to shout to her: 'Hey, Rimka, throw me your book over!' With her this tone was quite impossible. And I could not adopt another without risking the jeers of my classmates. They too, it must be said, also avoided being coarse and uncouth in their dealings with Ri – maybe because she was rather reserved and taciturn, and she herself never descended to a frivolous manner.

At the beginning of a new term there is the traditional revision of the previous year's work. When Ri answered well and obtained good marks, my heart swelled with pride. After all, I had taught her everything she knew!

But my heart stood still with fear whenever she hesitated before answering. On these occasions, she raised her eyebrows, holding them high; I knew this expression of hers, I remembered it well and could have cried each time I saw it writ on her face. I knew by heart each movement of her lips, her eyebrows, her every gesture, and I could guess unerringly all her moods, all her desires.

I so positioned myself in class that I could always see her face but could switch my gaze at any moment to the blackboard, the door, or the schoolmistress.

The trouble was that it simply was not enough to be able just to look at her; I wanted to see her eyes and used all kinds of cunning to this end. When the bell sounded I was first to run into the corridor and then, as if having forgotten something, would retrace my steps so as to meet her face to face. And whenever I succeeded in doing this, I felt something mysterious each time in my heart – like the feeling you get on a swing – and if by chance her eyes met mine, my heart brimmed over, choked with emotion.

When I met her on the stairs or in the corridor, I was engulfed by the strangest sensation – as though I had imbibed some potion of fear which coursed through my whole being, smothering me . . .

The hours that I spent at school were my whole life. After lessons when I had to return home, time seemed to stand still, transformed for the while into some kind of viscous plasma.

I began to detest Saturdays, for she went home each Saturday. Sundays became the days when life lost all meaning and was lived in vain. But Sunday evening was at once the most exciting and anguished time of the week. On Sunday evenings she would return, and I would wait at the window for her to pass our house. Perhaps she would not come; she might have missed her train or fallen ill; God alone knew what could have happened to her.

Between times the little worm of pain grew and grew till it turned into a young serpent.

At the start of term I worked hard, thinking I would die of shame in front of Ri if I obtained only a two.* But gradually I understood that it was a matter of total indifference to her whether I got a five or a two. And so I lost all interest in my studies.

It was Svetka who first began to laugh at me. Then the other girls followed suit. Later the boys began to look at me in a way I found insulting, though not actually unfair. Things went from bad to worse. Yurka once pulled the ribbon which tied Ri's hair and during the following break I fought fiercely with him.

Something even more terrible happened during the geography class. The teacher had told us in the previous lesson about the origin of Baikal, of how it had been formed fifteen million years before through a geological fault in a gap or a fissure, and so on. I was particularly indignant at these fifteen million years. The teacher spoke as if she could actually know what these fifteen million years had entailed. As if she could!

The next day she called me to the blackboard. At first I stood and said nothing. She repeated the question: 'Now then, how was Baikal formed exactly?'

'I don't know,' I replied rudely. 'Nor does anyone!'

'What do you mean, no one knows?' she asked,

* 'Two' means two out of a possible five, according to the marking system used in Russian educational establishments. [Tr.]

astonished. 'I told you yesterday that fifteen million years ago . . . '

'Did you count them, all these millions, or what?' I asked maliciously.

The teacher, still young for the job, was quite perplexed. I had never before been rude to her like that. Blinking, she said: 'Of course I didn't count them, but science can . . . '

'Science!' I scorned.

'Go to your place!'

The whole class looked at me in disbelief, including Ri; it was indeed painful to have to defend the legend.

What followed was even worse. The teacher called out Ri and put the same question to her.

'Fifteen million years ago . . . ' she began.

I couldn't stand it any longer. I banged the lid of my desk twice and shouted at the top of my voice: 'Quiet! Don't dare say that! Enough!'

The teacher, pale and with lips trembling, ordered me to leave the classroom. I had done the unspeakable – I had ruined the lesson!

What can I say about the consequences? Perhaps the saddest was that I really had not wanted to insult the teacher but she, imagining that I had done it all on purpose, spent the whole of the following lesson crying in the staffroom. I apologised of course, but that was hardly the point . . .

The only one to understand me was Friend. The next day after lessons, I took him to the school and waited for the boarders to come outside. Ri was among them. I bent down and whispered in the dog's ear: 'Look! There she is! Do you see her?'

Friend became quite agitated and wagged his tail, requesting permission to go up to her. I let him.

Ri was frightened and asked: 'He won't bite, will he?'

I only smiled. Friend stood on his hind legs, placing his front paws on Ri's shoulders, and licked her face.

I gave him a whistle, rushed off and began to clamber down the gorge. Friend caught up with me and for a long time we wrestled in the bushes and chased one another on the slope of the mountain, and then, still hugging one another, we lay down on a rock and both thought about the same thing.

During this time the little serpent of sadness became a fully grown snake. I could not live alongside Baikolla's daughter without talking to her; I had to say something if only to make her look at me from time to time or say a few words but, as time went on, it became harder to find a pretext for approaching her. My friend Genka began to borrow her jotter far too often for copying, as if he couldn't have found anyone else to ask! And Valerka as well! I saw with my own eyes during the botany lesson how he sent her a note. And Svetka, too, was guilty of a really low trick: she started calling me 'Rimka's sweetheart'.

On the other hand, none of my friends could really be blamed. They knew nothing after all, and simply thought I was head over heels in love. I would have got up to exactly the same tricks in their place.

Twice I climbed the crag and, after trying to avoid the sharp eye of Sarma (who in fact missed nothing), I spent a few hours with Baikolla, telling him all I could about his daughter.

On the first of October there was a violent storm to the north of Baikal which brought the Barguzin to us midst a huge swell, even though the day was warm and sunny and the wind only light.

After the second lesson we were taken for a medical examination to the clinic situated hard on the shore of Lake Baikal. After the medical we spilled out on to the beach – it was not every day you could see such waves. Ri stood on a high, pointed rock and surveyed the waves. She looked at them as if she remembered something. She strained forward, lips trembling, and one imagined that at any moment her arms would reach out towards whatever she saw in front of her or whatever provoked her memory . . . She was so beautiful at that moment, one could have looked at her and died. Forgetting everything, including my classmates all around, I climbed on to the rock with her, somehow found a foothold on the edge, and stood there beside her.

A wave swept against the rock and flew upwards, but, without reaching our feet, it toppled back and seemed to swallow itself, already crushed by the next wave, just as frenzied, just as hunchbacked. The waves were tinted brown, the water troubled, and there in the distance, above the lake, the lacerated black and grey clouds teased the waves and urged them on.

There was hardly any room on the rock and I was practically touching Ri's shoulders. The least breath of wind caused her hair to brush my face gently and I trembled all over, afraid of losing my balance. But she did not even notice that I stood next to her. She was staring so fixedly in front of her and so absorbed in her own thoughts that even if I had touched her hand, she would have felt nothing.

I was standing so close to her that, in spite of the rumble of the waves, I suddenly heard her utter one word, which she repeated several times: 'Barguzin! Barguzin!' she whispered, as if listening to the word, as if this was the word she could hear. And then, forgetting all Sarma's warnings, forgetting

157

everything, I pronounced the word in her ear as it was heard in the Valley of the Young Moon: 'Barguzzi!'

At that very moment, a wave struck Ri on the legs, whereupon she cried out, lost her balance, slid from the top of the rock and fell into the water. I managed to grab her by the hand, pull her on to the rock, where I saw her terrified eyes and her hand covered in blood. People were already running towards us and gathering round, and the schoolmistress took Ri in her arms and carried her to the clinic; only then did I manage to regain some composure. I shouted some oath at no one in particular and rushed off along the shore, leaping from rock to rock, risking broken legs in the process. Several times the waves swept over me but I took no notice.

After running a long way I reached the turning-off point where I could not be seen from the village; I stopped and screamed out madly: 'Damn it all! Damn it all!'

I seized a stone and hurled it on to the crest of a wave. The crest broke up, swallowed the stone and spat out its spume at me.

'Take that! And that!' I cried, beating the waves with staves. But the waves only laughed at me.

I sat down on a rock, buried my face in my hands and murmured, 'Bastard! Bastard!' I was disgusted with myself. I despised and detested myself.

'That's it! I can't take any more! I can't take it!' I cried out suddenly, and ran back to the village as quickly as my legs would carry me. I overtook my classmates returning to school and ran, or so it seemed, as far as Dead Man's Crag itself, chanting with each step as I climbed up: 'I've had enough! I can't take any more . . . ' And that's what I shouted to Sarma as soon as I spied her: 'I've had enough! That's it!'

'So you hurt her, you stupid little blabbermouth!' she exclaimed. 'Didn't I warn you? But you couldn't hold your tongue, could you? Well? Answer!'

'I couldn't help it!' I replied, swallowing my tears.

'Did you cause her much pain, then?'

'There was some blood . . . ' I whimpered, nose running.

'You spilled her blood!' cried Sarma, horrified. 'Well, then, go and find Baikolla, and make him happy by telling him how you are a friend of the people of the valley. Go!'

I shook my head.

'You're afraid! You're ashamed!'

'I can't take any more!' I repeated through my tears. 'I don't want any more! Let me forget everything!'

'Come closer!' said Sarma. 'And stop snivelling! Closer, I tell you, come closer!'

She took my hand and spoke in a soft, sad voice: 'Now then, you see. I warned you in advance that it wouldn't be easy, that the burden would be too great for you. You took upon yourself the pain and sadness of Baikolla's daughter; I did not have the right to do that to you and I will make amends. You will go from here and your life will once again become happy and peaceful.'

These words put me on my guard. 'And what about Ri? What will become of her?'

Sarma sighed. 'She will return to her father in the castle!'

'No!' I cried. 'No!'

'Why not? Wasn't that why you came here?'

'That's not fair!'

'What do you understand of fairness!' replied Sarma in a tired voice. 'And what am I to do with your sadness if I free you from it? Take it on myself? I'm already withering under my own. Perhaps you know what I could do with it? Grief, sadness, guilt – all these come from people and belong to people! Away with you!'

'No!'

'Yet another "no"? What's wrong now?'

I wiped my eyes with my shirt, looked hard at Sarma and said softly: 'Let everything be as it was before!'

She looked straight into my eyes. 'Believe me,' she said in a quite different voice, 'believe me, I just don't know what I can do with all the sadness. I can't just drown it or scatter it to the winds.'

'Let everything be as it was!' I repeated.

'That would be even more difficult for you. What if you harmed her again!'

'No! She will never be hurt again!'

'Well, it's up to you!'

'Can I simply . . . I don't want to say anything to Baikolla . . . '

'You don't have to,' she agreed. 'He is wretched enough as it is.'

'I'm going back!'

Suddenly she stroked my head, just as old Vassina had done.

The next day at the first break Ri came up to me, her hand all bandaged.

'You saved me yesterday, thank you.'

'There's nothing to thank me for,' I replied bitterly.

'But it was you who . . . '

'I didn't save you! Understand that, I didn't save you!'

'But you . . . ' She shrugged her shoulders and wandered off. And I flew like the wind out into the playground.

That night I dreamed I was beside Baikolla's daughter,

high up on a crag overlooking Lake Baikal. She was so beautiful, so indescribably beautiful . . . I stood very close and suddenly kissed her on the cheek. She blenched and fell from the cliff. All the boys and girls danced around shouting: 'He kissed her! He kissed her!' I threw stones at them and screamed: 'It's not true! I didn't! I didn't!'

At this point I woke up and heard myself still whispering: 'It's not true! It's not true! I didn't kiss her . . . '

6

BAIKAL BLAZED WITH COLOUR for only a short time before being covered by frost and then snow. It melted, of course, and disappeared after two days, but not before changing the complexion of autumn. Cold winds, bringing rain and dampness, whistled up and down the gorge. And Lake Baikal was permanently stormy. It was never pale blue now, even on clear days; most often it was a leaden grey and only when the Kultuk swell came with its foamy peaks was it a dark, dark blue.

On Baikal, the second half of autumn is the saddest season of the year: cold rains and cold winds on a severe, ungracious lake.

The second snow fell and did not melt; this marked the onset of winter. The little stream that flowed down the gorge took on a mantle of ice, but the water, not quite believing in the face of winter, burst through where it could, and positively leapt from rock to rock. One night, however, it stopped in its tracks and by morning it was frozen in a glistening blanket of ice. And that was surely a miracle. For how could one have imagined that the flow of the stream could be halted and frozen solid?

Winter was taking a grip all round and everything became white; except the green of the fir trees and cedars on the slopes, but that was a dim green, so much so that it hardly counted as green any more and appeared simply as a dark patch on the white.

Only Lake Baikal, its shores dressed in white, kept – at

least on sunny days – something of its dark-blue tones. Storms swept from one shore to another and along its banks and it seemed as if Baikal was so cold that it stormed in order to get warm. Long white antennae crept along its sandy banks but the lake itself was still strong enough to resist the frost which was ultimately too weak to get the better of the lake.

For the boys there began a new joy – skating. Skates were attached to the boots with string but of course no string could hold out when they skated all day long, as they did on Sundays for example. That is why they would quickly plunge the boot with the skate attached quickly into the water, then hold it for some time in snow so that the skates adhered to the boots. This method weighed heavily on the legs but it was reliable none the less.

The whole uninhabited area from Dead Man's Crag to the banks of the Baikal was covered with ice. We would go up the gorge as far as the fork and slide all the way down, sometimes without stopping, sometimes falling into a crevice where we'd play 'sacks in the mill' by piling on to one another, spinning and floundering before sliding to the bottom where we'd put on our skates once again and fly like the wind on to the icy banks of the Baikal.

Or sometimes we would knock three planks together and fix them on three skates, two behind and one in front for steering. Several children would lie on this contraption and career down the gorge to the lake.

On Sundays and in the evenings the din from the children playing echoed through the whole valley and this was the noisiest and happiest time in the life of the whole village.

And my life? I led, so to speak, a double life: one when I was with my friends, the other when I found myself alone.

Of course I did not actually let any of the early winter joys pass me by . . . I skated till late in the evening just like the others, gasped for breath under the onslaught of snowballs, rolled head over heels in the frozen gullies on the slopes of the gorge, and took part in all the other activities which filled the free hours outside the classroom.

In all our games, moreover, I tended to be the most adventurous and daring – even to the point of sheer madness – and it was rare for anyone to return home after me, because going home, for me, signified a return to everything which constituted my second life.

The days and the weeks went past and there was no change in my relations with the girl from Dead Man's Crag. In fact, it would be more accurate to say that there was no relationship at all.

She – the subject of all my thoughts – lived her own life, known only to her; it passed mine by, like a distant cutter which glides past the shoreline without sailing to harbour.

Ri had forgotten everything, whereas I could not forget anything. I could not forget those days when her voice had sounded like music to my ears, when we had looked into each other's eyes, as lovers do, when we knew everything about each other, and this knowledge belonged to us alone.

If she had been an ordinary girl like the others, our dealings could have been simple and straightforward; I could have written her a note and asked her to be my friend, as Valerka had done. But this I could not do for a multitude of reasons, one being that though I dreamed of being friends with her, I nevertheless feared to be left alone with her, to have our eyes meet, even for a minute. For I could not regard her as I could any other girl; she was, for me, Baikolla's daughter and I could not be certain that, by word or allusion, quite unintended, I would not remind her of the past. And to have seen tears in her eyes once again would, for me, have been equal to dying.

The way the children greeted each other at school changed quite unexpectedly. One day when I went to school, instead of the customary 'Hullo!' to those I met on the way – this sometimes took the form of tripping up the other person, or throwing a snowball – the greeting became the more formal 'Good day!' I do not know how this fashion started, because no one forced us to greet each other in this way, but it had the subsequent effect of providing a moment's happiness each day. The morning after this new greeting caught on, I arrived at school a little earlier than the others (I had waited impatiently for this moment) and when I saw Ri walking in the corridor with someone I hid and waited for the right opportunity to greet her. When I said 'Good day!', she most definitely looked at me and returned the 'Good day!' and those two words alone, spoken only for me, seemed to give me giant wings and carry me up into the air.

Each new day she seemed to pronounce the words better than the day before; they began to sound friendly and even sincere. I tried to hear how she greeted the other boys and thought her tone with them was actually colder; and the consequent ray of hope which was planted in my heart was so sweet that my desire to live was more intense than ever before.

During the school breaks I never played outside or ran about in the corridor, for I had no time for those things; as a rule I would stand somewhere near Ri with my back to her, and straining my whole body, not only my ears, I would listen for her voice above all the other voices.

It was strange that no one had remarked on the extra-ordinary quality of her voice. The first time she spoke I was even quite afraid that someone would draw attention to it, and ask why she sounded as she did, for such a question could have provoked some memory in her and caused her pain.

My heart used to thump loudly each time I saw her looking sad or pensive, for each time I imagined she was going to remember something. I would even try to guess what it could be and catch myself embarking on the perilous desire to say something, as I had done before with such dire consequences.

Sometimes I could almost see and feel a kind of treachery in the fact that she remembered nothing: infidelity to Baikolla and everything connected with the story of the valley, and even a measure of infidelity towards me.

This thought was, of course, unjust – I understood that; but to censure one's thoughts was not the same as being able to get rid of them.

Gradually my classmates' attitude towards me began to change in an interesting way. Previously, whenever they had tittered or dropped hints, I simply paid no attention. I certainly didn't fall out with them and I soon even stopped noticing altogether. But one day when I had arrived at the cinema a little after the others, Svetka, who had been keeping a place for me, called me over. When I sat down Svetka had disappeared and Ri was in her place. Of course I can recall nothing about the film which was shown that day.

Then Yurka, with whom I had had a fight at some point, came and suggested that we make it up and gave me some splendid strings for my skates. And Genka, who for some time had held me in contempt, took hold of a boy who had made some snide remark at me and pinned him up against the wall.

But our teacher, Tatyana Ivanovna, who came to visit us on one occasion, asked me casually if it might be better for me to move my place in class from the middle to the first row of desks. She and Mother exchanged looks. I blushed and refused. No, it would not be better. For then I would not have been able to look at Ri during the lessons.

The winter holidays drew near and I contemplated them with horror. Ri would have to go away for two weeks and I could not imagine how I would survive that length of time without her. It was then that a brilliant idea came into my head. I thought it over for several days till one day I made it happen. I asked Svetka to bring some of her photographs to school. She brought the one of her standing next to the dead bear. The photograph did the rounds during the next two breaks and at the third, plucking up all my courage and summoning all my strength to remain calm, I went up to Ri and asked her casually: 'Have you ever been photographed?'

I was certain that she had not (for when could it have happened?) and my plan was to make her want to be photographed. But her reply took me by surprise: 'Why, of course I have!'

I was aghast. I had prepared a long and difficult mission which had been rendered futile at a stroke. I quite lost my head and said hoarsely: 'Why don't you bring it then?'

She looked at me, lowered her eyes and said: 'All right.'

I walked to the door of the classroom quite normally but once in the corridor I reeled with joy; it was only Wednesday – how could I survive until the following Monday!

But survive I did. And instead of the fashionable 'Good day!' I quickly asked her in nervous tones: 'Did you bring it?'

She opened her school bag and took out her diary, from which she removed a photograph. She gave it to me. I took it casually, thrust it into my own school bag, and went outside again.

I missed the first lesson which was something unheard of at the school, but I couldn't have cared less!

Now, as I write this, I have in front of me that same faded photograph of a twelve-year-old girl – five years younger than my own daughter – and I cannot begin to explain the feeling of sweet sorrow that engulfs me.

I have lived – and continue to live – an interesting life; that much I can say without exaggeration. But if I imagined for a minute that everything in these pages describing my childhood had not taken place, then my life would lose all its colour and I would be left with the impression of having lived under an overcast sky without ever having seen the sun, and without any sign of that pure light whose warm, sad beam has accompanied me throughout life's tortuous paths.

For some time everything changed. Ri was always with me. I could look at her as much as I wanted. I could talk to her about what she had forgotten, about what she was not meant to remember. And I was happy.

One Sunday around this time, I went into the drop. Snow covered the stony ground in front of Dead Man's Crag, making it terribly difficult to reach; as for climbing, that seemed to be out of the question. But I climbed all the same, even though it took me five times as long as it usually did.

Sarma was in her usual place, sitting all wrapped up in something warm and fluffy, her hands hidden in a large muff of the same material.

I showed her the photograph and described Ri's life among the people; she listened attentively and looked for a long time at the photograph.

'The people have learned to leave a memory of themselves on paper,' she said, shaking her head. 'But have they not forgotten how to leave a memory in the heart?'

I did not know what to answer her.

'People grow old and die. The mirror reflects a moment in time and has the value of the instantaneous just as the truth of the image reflected is instantaneous. Only the great deeds of men are eternal. But do people understand the difference between the eternal and the merely instantaneous?'

I was silent.

'Don't go to Baikolla! He ought not to see that!'

She gave the photograph back to me and I looked into her eyes.

'Forgive Baikolla. How many more years can this go on?'

'You've understood nothing!' she said angrily. 'I don't know how to forgive! I don't know how!'

'What do you mean, you don't know how? Forgive him, and be done with it!'

'Go away!' she ordered. 'Baikolla this, Baikolla that! And yet you show no such respect for me! Do you have any idea of how *I* suffer, you silly little boy? Get away with you!'

I stayed a little longer, but soon I began to feel frozen to the bone; the wind at such a height – though not particularly strong – was icy cold. And I was afraid of catching a chill, for the climb had made me sweat.

As I went away the thought in my mind was that I would

be in no hurry to return, because there is nothing worse in the world than to feel helpless when faced with the unhappiness of others.

Each day after school towards the end of December I would race to Lake Baikal. Everyone said that soon it would ice over, though it was somehow impossible to believe that it would. The lake at that time was a uniform colour – blue-black; how could one imagine that this blue-black would turn white, the colour of ice?

I did not believe I would see Baikal covered in ice, nor did I want to. There seemed to be something almost unjust in it. But I could already feel in my bones that it was inevitable, foretold partly by the spray from the waves which was cold and biting, like splinters of ice, and partly by the white foam which resembled icicles sitting astride the black sheets of water. Above all, the winds and the white mists over Baikal seemed to chain the lake to an earth which already slept under a blanket of white.

On one of the crags where Friend and I had spent a lot of time together the previous summer, there was a little fir tree which stood on a ledge about two metres above the water. When I went back one day to this place, the entire tree was wreathed in crystal and garlands of pearls. This was how the December frost had dealt with the spray from the waves. All the rocks at the foot of the crags were also glazed with ice and sparkled like mirrors, reflecting the waves, the sky and the summits of the overhanging peaks.

Then a storm blew up over Baikal. Baikal worked hard. I tried to make sense of this effort. Was the lake fighting against the cold, or was it possible to detect in the frantic, gloomy rush of water an indefinable haste, as if Lake Baikal were rushing to complete some task which it had started but not managed to finish? I understood and felt close to Baikal in all its forms but for some reason the preoccupied gloom of the icy blue expanse caught my heart and awoke a passionate sympathy.

Every morning when I left for school the first thing I did was to cast my eyes under the bridge from where one could see Lake Baikal, and great indeed was my joy when I saw that it still had not capitulated, and I would wave my hand, signalling my promise to return soon, to give encouragement and just to be there, for I knew the pain of loneliness at a time of important decisions and difficult deeds.

On leaving the banks of Baikal to go home in the evening, I would say to the lake: 'Now, just you hold on! The essential thing is to hold out until morning!'

Later, it turned out that I had been right. It was precisely at night that the lake had weakened and decided to take a little rest, whereupon the ice had chained its sleepy waters. Waking the following morning to its tough blanket of ice, Baikal in places found the necessary strength to tear it to shreds and throw it on to its shores. But this struggle sapped it of its resources, and the following night, the frost, having waited for its moment to strike, dressed the lake in a coat of armour; in the morning, its embrace, far from weakening, turned into the grip of death, and finally Baikal surrendered.

On that day – the last of the year – when Ri was to leave for the inconceivably long period of two weeks, Lake Baikal was particularly troubled. I arrived at the station long before the train was due and stood there remembering the New Year celebrations of the previous evening. Ri had worn a party dress and the crescent of the young moon had sparkled in her hair. She had seemed to be observing the moon very closely, and I was afraid lest she remembered something she should not. She was indescribably beautiful that evening. We all played 'postman', that is, each child had a number on his chest and the postman had to deliver everyone's notes. I resolved to write: 'You are more beautiful than your sister', alluding to Ngara, Baikolla's elder daughter, of whose beauty Ri had told me so often.

'But I have only a brother, aged two!' was how Ri answered me. To avoid appearing stupid, I quickly tore the number from my chest so that perhaps she wouldn't realise that I had written the note. But as she walked past me, she gave me a knowing smile and I hid in shame among the other boys.

In those moments before the train arrived, I felt troubled and sad and even more in sympathy with the anxious rush of the Baikal waves. I felt an urge to turn to the lake as I would to a friend, to call it by its name, to touch it lightly on the hand or cheek, as if we belonged to the same species . . .

In front of the carriage I went up to Ri and said: 'Goodbye!' She held out her hand to me, and I touched it for the first time. From this moment, from the time she cast me her farewell look, I knew that the fortnight ahead would be an incomparable trial. But I consoled myself with the thought that everything afterwards would be different, and it was with this growing presentiment of joy that I spent the entire holiday – apart from my accident which was to be remembered by the locals for a very long time.

One morning, as I went out on to the porch, I felt a change in the weather and guessed that the wind had dropped. I went down the steps and, glancing as usual under the bridge, I did not see Lake Baikal, but in its place a brilliant, sparkling, dazzling expanse. When I ran to the shore I found boys already there, throwing stones on to the thin film of ice which shattered at each direct hit, allowing the water to gush through the holes. The ice was flawless and smooth as a mirror, and the mirror itself was infinite.

'We'll be able to skate tomorrow!' shouted Valerka. I did not believe him. The ice was only the thickness of a finger.

The following morning, however, there was not a boy to be seen on the river, so I skated along as far as the lake where I stopped in amazement. Like little black dots the boys rushed up and down the length of the lake. I was afraid even to put one foot on the ice for it was quite transparent and the bottom of the lake was now almost visible.

The boys skated up to me and dragged me on to the ice which, to my horror, began to cave in beneath my feet. But it did not actually break, it only sagged.

'Don't be afraid!' Yurka called to me. 'You'll see. It will take your weight all right!'

As if to demonstrate, he sat down on the ice, raised his leg in the air and struck the ice with the heel of his skate. Water immediately began to pour through the hole he'd punched, and I made a headlong dash for the shore, accompanied by loud laughter from the other boys.

With a scowl, I advanced gingerly in their direction once more.

'Come on! Don't be afraid!' shouted one of them, and all together they began to skate further and further from the shore. I followed, trying not to lean too heavily on my skates, as if this would somehow diminish my actual weight.

But everyone's fate is predetermined, or so it is said. I

was almost beginning to feel at home and had almost ceased to be afraid of the strange softness of the ice and the depths which glittered beneath my feet. I was skating in front of Valerka at full speed, parallel to the shore. Suddenly I saw in front of me a patch of ice which seemed clearer than the rest and a little distended. I did not have time either to become anxious or to avoid it; I merely jumped over it and ground to a halt.

I turned round to say something to Valerka – I wanted to ask him why the ice was like that, but he just opened his eyes wide, shouted out something which I did not understand, and skated off in the opposite direction.

I automatically began to follow him but suddenly there was a crack beneath my skates. At first I sank only up to my shins and for a fraction of a second seemed to stick there before I was plunged into the water up to my ears. This happened about a hundred metres from the shore. I was wearing heavy snowboots with skates attached, and a thick sheepskin jacket with several layers underneath (I had meant to stay out for the whole day).

According to all the rules, I was doomed. The ice was only a thin film on the water and supported our weight because of the general tension on it, but once having fallen into a 'bubble' – as these holes were called – it was impossible to climb back on to the ice which simply broke at a touch like a thin pane of glass; my only prospect was to break it all the way to the shore – an impossible task, not only because my strength was limited, but because the cold was already producing body cramps.

The other boys had already skated ashore. This did not amount to betrayal; they simply knew what the ice was like. They dared not come even within ten metres of me. I cannot say what they were feeling, but as for me, I felt absolutely nothing – or so it seemed. Floundering in the water, I stabbed the ice with both hands and, as far as I remember, screamed quietly.

Later, and for many years after that, when I was asked how I managed to get out of the situation, I had to invent a version to satisfy general curiosity. I said that when I broke the ice I discovered another layer beneath which took my weight and enabled me to scramble out.

People like nothing less than not being able to understand something; indeed they prefer not to know. And so, in defiance of all logic, they swallowed this utterly absurd explanation without even inquiring how this second layer of ice could have been formed on only the second day of freezing.

But now I am able to tell what really happened. After smashing an area of ice about seven metres in width, I was still whimpering and struggling desperately when suddenly at the very edge of the ice in front of me Sarma appeared.

'Why are you whining, little coward!' she said indignantly. 'Haven't I already told you that as long as you live on these shores nothing will ever happen to you! So stop your snivelling at once! It's offensive to the ears! Give me your hand!'

I held out my hand to her but I could not feel hers. She seemed remote, intangible, and I simply stretched out towards her and was carried away after her.

'Don't fuss!' shouted Sarma angrily. 'Swim on the ice! Swim! Don't crush it with your elbows!'

The ice sagged under my weight, but it did not break.

'Now crawl! Crawl! Don't lean on your elbows! Don't drag your feet! Crawl!'

Sarma moved gradually towards the shore and I wormed my way along behind her for what seemed like a very long time until she said: 'That's enough! Get up and run home as fast as you can!'

The boys on the shore greeted me like a spirit from another world. People ran towards me with Uncle Seryozha in front. He grabbed me in his arms and ran home with me to his house which was nearer than ours. There I was undressed, rubbed all over with vodka, dressed again and wrapped up in blankets before being put in a huge bed and being made to drink half a glass of vodka, which practically gave me convulsions.

Shortly afterwards Mother came running to Seryozha's house. She smacked me, embraced me, kissed me, then began to cry and say over and over again: 'Why does it always have to be you? First you're caught in an avalanche, then you fall through the ice! What does it all mean? Has someone put the evil eye on you, or what?'

But Sarma had spoken true and I did not even catch a cold. My friends had taken Sarma to be old Vassina and described how she had pulled me over the ice; but, of course, they lied, for things had happened quite differently.

These events gave rise to long deliberations on my part regarding the extent of the protection granted me by Sarma. It seemed to open up immense possibilities which I finally decided to put to the test.

On the right-hand slope of the gorge, almost directly above the school, there was a crag about fifteen metres high. Beneath the crag there was a little ledge laden with snow, which I decided I would jump into from the top of the crag. No one would even have considered attempting such a jump in the normal course of events. For although there was snow to break one's fall, it was still a considerable height, and one would have hesitated to jump from that height into water, far less snow.

I climbed the crag and squatted on the edge from where the altitude seemed even greater. To say that it was terrifying was a grave understatement. Several times I stood up but each time sat down again like a coward; thus, I spent nearly an hour on the crag. When, at last, I came down without having jumped, it was with sadness and some chagrin that I understood the fact that Sarma's gift in no way supplemented what I myself was able to do, and this discovery upset me for a long time.

My story is nearing its end – an end which, if one allows for the feelings of a twelve-year-old boy, is necessarily a sad one. But when I recall this sadness and describe it, it is as if I am also touching on a happiness which I was unable to appreciate fully at the time, but which even now has lost neither its warmth nor its sparkle.

The entire holiday period passed in anticipation of a change in my relationship with Baikolla's daughter. I could in no way imagine how it ought to change; I neither knew nor understood what it was I wanted. Indeed, I knew only one thing: I would not and could not remain a stranger for her, nor did I want simply to be like one of the others. But I could not fail to recognise that a true friendship between us was possible only on the basis of everything which had connected us before, everything she had forgotten irrevocably.

What, then, could I hope for? When I look back, it seems that I did not think of anything concrete at all; I simply imagined that when the holidays came to an end, Ri would come back to Marituy and there would no longer be that invisible wall dividing us. This would all come about quite spontaneously; we would look into each other's eyes simply and sincerely as we had done in the castle when Ri had told me the legend and I had taught her my lessons. But when I met her from the train and said 'Good day!', she simply answered and went on her way, as if nothing had happened, nothing had changed – in other words, we were still strangers, now and for ever, and the realisation of this drained the life out of me . . .

Everything would be the same as before. I would have to start the business all over again of looking at her during the lessons, eavesdropping during the breaks, lying in wait for her at the station – and why, for what? This terrible 'why' was so unanswerable, so irresolvable, so impossible, that even to hear or pronounce the word was like a fallen log blocking a path, collapsing on the very essence of life's meaning.

From then on, I walked to school as I would have marched into purgatory; at breaktime I stayed in the class-room or ran about behind the school; after school, I sat for hours with my school books without so much as looking at them. In the evenings I would go with Friend into the gorge and wander around the foot of Dead Man's Crag without any intention of climbing up. Friend looked at me anxiously, trying to distract me, to cheer me up, but I played with him only for his sake and without deriving any pleasure from our games.

I eventually finished reading the sad story about the son of the last of the Mohicans, who died saving the one he loved, and in my imagination I was carried away by ever more tragic tales in which I died saving Ri. All the stories ended up with my death, even though only shortly before, my fantasies had reached quite a different conclusion. This was a measure of how the whole world had changed for me.

I became very bad at my studies and this had immediate repercussions at home, particularly with Mother. Her reproaches did not really upset me; I only felt sorry for her because I was powerless to change anything.

I reached the stage of going to school in the evenings when no one was there, sitting at Ri's desk and weeping, without knowing why, like the worst crybaby.

The opportunity to die in the act of saving Ri did not present itself. I did not want to go on living, but at the same time I did not want to die for nothing. My days passed in anticipation of some event which would decide my fate. The occasion was my birthday.

In later years I learned that it was ill-advised to recognise one's thirteenth birthday. This, no doubt, is superstitious nonsense, but the fact remains that mine turned out badly.

In the evening, as custom dictates, there was cake and presents and felicitations, but that day at school I had once again obtained a two and to have received that mark on such a day when I could easily have done so much better was taken by Mother as a personal offence. Since she was unable to conceal her feelings, the whole evening passed off with great tension, even though Father did his best to keep up the festive mood.

Mother could not keep herself in check, however, and began to scold me gently for my conduct. I replied rather cheekily, Mother burst into tears and things went from bad to worse. Towards the end Mother said that never in all her wildest dreams had she imagined that one day she would have to feel ashamed of her own son.

This was understandable: I was, after all, the son of two teachers.

I went to my room, lay on my bed and knew at that moment that the end of my torment was nigh, that I wanted to live no longer. I had no intention of doing anything terrible to myself – I knew another method of putting an end to my life.

I waited till the middle of the night, got up, dressed and went outside. The night was amazingly bright. A full moon hung in the clear sky over the gorge and that, together with the snow, threw out such a strong light all around that it seemed as if dawn had already broken.

Friend came out of his kennel and I held him tight in my arms. I did not want to take him with me; he had to live after all – that was why Baikolla had given him to me. I bade him farewell and made my way towards the drop. Here and there dogs, alarmed by the sound of my footsteps, shattered the silence of the night with their barking, but they quickly settled down again. In our part of the world, there were no strangers roaming about in the night.

I approached the school and stood there looking up at the windows where the boarders slept, and at one window in particular – that of Ri's bedroom. I said in a whisper: 'This is the end. We won't see each other any more, though for you it's unimportant. I don't regret having held out my hand to the serpent. In general, I don't regret anything at all. The essential thing is that Baikolla's daughter should live. And now I am able, albeit in a small way, to help Baikolla also. Goodbye, girl from Dead Man's Crag, or rather, farewell!'

I do believe that what I said then was really much more beautiful than the words I have written now, but it is difficult after so many years to preserve and reproduce the tragic, solemn tones of valediction. But what I said was certainly sincere, for in the depths of my soul I no longer retained the desire to live.

I continued into the drop. In the silence of the night the snow crunched so loudly underfoot that I was afraid of waking all the invisible and unknown creatures that slept beneath the snow, in the trees and under the rocks. Sometimes it struck me that the noise came not from my own footsteps but from someone following me and I would spin round quickly, pleased that the night was so clear. But in general I had no fear. Fear of what, in any case? Afterwards, however – even as much as a month later – whenever I recalled this nocturnal episode, my blood would run ice-cold.

I walked, crawled and fought my way through the fallen, snow-covered rocks at the foot of Dead Man's Crag, confident that nothing could happen which had not been provided for in my plan. Besides, I knew by heart each step, each foothold, so that even had the night been pitch-dark, I could still have made the climb without putting a foot wrong.

But however bright the night was, I saw nothing of Sarma (who was not in her usual place) till her shouts made me jump.

'Have you gone quite mad? Treading all over my feet! This boy has quite taken leave of his senses, that's for sure! Scrambling about on the crag in the middle of the night!'

'I'm sorry . . . ' I stuttered, 'I came . . . '

'You came because you're crazy! You get worse and worse! And you've hurt my foot, you little troublemaker!'

'I have come for always,' I said when she had stopped shouting. 'I've had enough of life!'

'So . . . that's it!' she drawled. 'So that's the stage we're at! You have come to know the full measure of sadness at last! Well, you can't say I didn't warn you! And so what are you planning to do about it? Do you want to forget everything?'

'No,' I answered quickly. 'I want Ri to live, but I don't want to go on any more. I want to go to Baikolla and stay there with him . . . '

'Well now!' said Sarma in astonishment, 'so you don't want to live? Do you understand what that means?'

I was silent.

'No, I can't let you do it. You simply don't understand what you're saying. If you were to sit by Baikolla, you would forget about your world and all those whom you know and love. You would be left with only one feeling – the sadness of non-existence . . . '

I did not understand Sarma's words, nor did I want to listen; I simply wanted to put an end to living as quickly as possible.

'Even if you prevent me from going to Baikolla,' I interrupted, 'I won't go back home at any cost!'

'Can this really be so?' said Sarma in hushed tones. 'Is it really possible that the place of grief cannot remain empty? Then everything you have done up till now will have been in vain, which means I was right after all!'

'I'm freezing here! Let me go to Baikolla!'

Sarma was about to argue, but I was sick of all her talk.

'Very well,' she said, 'go to him. But I shall have to ponder the situation a while . . . '

'My daughter . . . has something happened to her?' asked Baikolla anxiously when he saw me.

182

'No, no,' I reassured him. 'She's alive . . . and well. I have come to you for ever.'

'For ever?'

'From now on, I shall be with you.'

I approached the throne and made to sit down. But Baikolla stopped me with his hand. 'Child, do you understand what you are doing?'

'I don't want to live!' I shouted, quite worn out.

I brushed aside his hand and sat down on Ri's throne.

Sometimes it happens that you fall asleep for just a moment and on waking it is as if you have slept for a very long time, as if you have had a dream lasting the whole night. And it can happen the other way round too. You can sleep the whole night through without any dreams and on waking think that you have hardly slept at all, merely dropped off for a moment.

It was something like that which happened to me. As soon as I touched the throne I had the sensation of falling through the air and I only just managed to grope for Baikolla's hand before my head lolled uncontrollably on to it. I was not dead, but neither was I alive. I lost all feelings, though I could still feel my own body; I had no sense of time and it was as though I had been transported to a point where neither time nor space existed, only self-knowledge. Nothing happened, and nothing impinged on my consciousness, for time had ceased to exist and the difference between the momentary and the eternal had disappeared.

I had the impression when I opened my eyes that less than a second had gone by, and was therefore astonished to see Friend standing in front of me – the more so as I'd left him tied up in his kennel. He pulled me from the throne by my coat and I could not understand what was happening.

'Sarma is calling you,' said Baikolla. 'Something must have happened up there!'

I was quite unable to get up from the throne, having no desire to leave it, but Friend literally dragged me by the coat. Immediately it was as if life poured on to me and into me, ideas – still unclear and inarticulate – bombarded my brain, and all the feelings, ignored through familiarity for so long, seemed to awaken and start shouting, to a point which deafened and blinded.

I understood only that I had to leave the castle, and from the way Friend was fretting, I guessed I had to go quickly. When I emerged from the cave I was amazed to be dazzled by the sun since I still had the impression I had sat on the throne for only a moment, but to judge from the sun's position, it was already afternoon.

'Hurry!' cried Sarma. 'Your father is climbing the crag to look for you. The climb is very dangerous for him, he might fall. Quickly! I'll close the entrance myself.'

That would be all I needed! For Father to fall to his death because of me. I scrambled down at top speed and it was Sarma's power alone which saved me from breaking my neck a dozen times. Even Friend caught me by the sleeve in places where I might have faltered. I saw my father down below, fighting his way up to a snow-covered ledge and my head reeled with fear for his safety.

'Papa! Papa!' I screamed. 'I'm coming! Don't climb up any further! I'm coming!'

But as soon as he saw me he waved and hurried towards me, dislodging stones and snow as he went. I practically somersaulted down the last bit and fell straight into his arms. As if in disbelief at having found me, he spoke in a voice hoarse and broken: 'You're alive! My son! Alive!'

But why should I have been dead?

'You're frozen, aren't you? You're frozen!' he repeated, feeling my face and hands. I did not immediately grasp the reason for his anxiety but then I realised that he believed I had spent the whole night out on the crag, in which case, of course, I would have been frozen stiff!

He took me in his arms, hoping no doubt to warm me up, though in fact I was sweating from the descent and longed to unbutton my coat and take off my hat. As we went down, he held my hand, or at least that is how he imagined it; in reality I held his, and prevented him from stumbling, for I knew every inch of the way down and where all the obstacles were concealed by the snow.

At home it was all tears, embraces, kisses. The doctor arrived, examined me for a long time and was as surprised as everyone else that I had not frozen to death. I explained that I had lit a wood fire and spent the whole night by it.

Often people do not need to be told the whole truth but simply require a minimal explanation of what they have no hope of understanding. That is why they believed me when I said that I had been saved by a wood fire; it never occurred to anyone that on Dead Man's Crag there are no trees, apart from the pine on its summit, and no one thought to ask just how much wood one would have needed to spend a whole night on the crag exposed to the four winds in temperatures of twenty degrees below!

From this day on there was not a murmur on the subject of my studies. If ever I got a two, Mother would simply say I ought to apply myself a little better to improve my grade.

This I would do and when I got a three, Mother would be happy.

Sometimes I could not find the strength to go to school and, unable to force myself, would declare that I was ill. Everyone immediately endorsed my illness and I was even allowed to stay at home the following day as well. But even at home one thing was unbearable, and whenever I got the sudden urge to see Ri again I would run back to school in time for the second or third class.

The presence of Ri in my life began to turn into a real torment. I quivered when I heard her voice or accidentally caught her eye, but I still could not live a single day without seeing her or hearing her. For months now I had not exchanged more than ten sentences with her and I began to understand more and more clearly that I was behaving wrongly, that I had adopted a stupid line of conduct which was constituting an obstacle, even in our most simple and straightforward dealings. But there was nothing I could do to alter this.

I lost all interest in boyish things and little by little a vacuum was formed around me. Even this did not distress me unduly.

A doctor came from Slyudyanka. He was a funny, bald man who asked me stupid questions, tapped me on the knee and ran his finger round my nose. He concluded that I was suffering from nervous exhaustion.

Mother and he whispered for a long time in the kitchen but I was too lethargic even to eavesdrop. When I finally did go to the door I heard the doctor click his tongue and say: 'You'd never think it could happen to a thirteen-year-old!'

'It just goes to show!' answered Mother sadly.

I guessed that they were saying something absurd about

me once again; they could not very well say anything sensible for they did not know anything.

Then it was spring, which I can recall only by its colours and smells. I remember the scarlet bands of wild rosemary on the northern slope of the gorge, and the smell of the little streams running down from all the shallow gullies into the gorge. I remember the yellow snowdrop which Ri held in her hand and the first day of the thaw on Lake Baikal; it looked sleepy, lazy and practically colourless.

But most of all I remember the pain which ousted all else from my memory during the fourteenth spring of my life.

And when Father announced that we were going away from Marituy, I received the news with some relief, although naturally without much joy. My father had been made director of another Siberian railway school, but Siberia is so vast that simply by moving from one place to another within Siberia one could cover distances which might not be repeated in a lifetime of travelling.

The school year drew to a close and the day arrived when Ri was to go home for the whole summer. I already knew that I would be seeing her for the last time and as we walked from the school to the station I held her hand, which she did not try to withdraw, perhaps sensing that we were about to part for ever . . .

I wanted to say something special to her, but I could not mention anything to do with Dead Man's Crag and had no desire to prattle aimlessly. So we went along in silence. We stood side by side waiting for the train; no one disturbed us, no one approached us.

When the train came, I said to her: 'I will always remember you.'

She lowered her eyes and did not answer. Perhaps it was a matter of indifference to her whether I remembered her or not.

Friend, who was by me, also went up to her and put his paws on her shoulders, whining softly. But she was afraid of him and I could only imagine how much this upset him. Then she climbed up the step, went into the carriage . . . and that was the end.

I never again saw the girl from Dead Man's Crag.

For the move we were once again given our own waggon and while our things were being loaded I ran off to say my goodbyes to all those I knew and loved in the village.

With Genka I visited White Grandad's grave. Then Yurka and I went off to find old Vassina.

'You are a fine boy,' said the old woman, 'and that is good. But you are also proud, and that is bad.'

I had never considered myself proud, but even if I were, would that be such a bad thing?

'A man is proud because he fears what people might say about him.'

'But I have no fear!' I objected, proudly.

She smiled. 'Well, that's splendid! God be with you!'

And I waited while she stroked my head and knew that I would never forget the touch of her hand.

With Svetka and Valerka I went on to the mountain. Svetka had managed to get a handful of caps from her father and we set them off with stones, then threw the stones down the mountain. I gave Valerka *The Last of the Mohicans* and he gave me his three-bladed penknife.

After dinner I went to bid farewell to Sarma and Baikolla. I dreaded this particular leave-taking. But having clambered up the first few ledges I was amazed to discover that the approach to the next foothold was barred. On the rock on to which I would normally have scrambled, there remained only a dark footprint. I searched in vain for a way round, but there was no gap, no access, which meant either that Sarma (who, after all, knew everything) had been offended by my departure, or that she was one of these people who could not suffer valediction.

I sat at the foot of Dead Man's Crag for about half an hour and, on leaving, I shouted out several times: 'Sarma! Forgive Baikolla! Forgive Baikolla!'

The echo was my only answer.

For the hour before the departure of our train, I bade my farewell to Lake Baikal. That day it looked almost exactly the same as when I had seen it for the first time – light blue, peaceful and scintillating. Only the mist was absent, and the mountains on the far shore stood out clearly and distinctly.

I said: 'Farewell, Baikal!' and tried to detect an answer in the barely perceptible movement of blue on its mirror-like surface.

'Farewell for ever!' But Baikal seemed to narrow its eyes artfully, as if not quite believing this 'for ever', almost as if it knew something about me which I did not yet know myself.

On that last day, strange though it may seem, I was granted an inner peace; the sadness of parting was without pain, which I perceived as a sign of new joys to come. One final sorrow awaited me, however.

We were already on the train, our things all packed away for the journey, and the guard came along shouting 'All on board!' The waggons gave a shudder, then another, the wheels began to scrape and the countryside began to drift slowly by, abandoning us to the movement of the train and me to my own peace of mind.

Suddenly, just as the train was getting up speed, Friend leapt up, began to whine and rush about the waggon. I called him and tried to grab his collar, but he broke loose, jumped up on Father, then on Mother, licking their hands; then he turned to me and licked my face all over, and with a last desperate whimper, jumped from the train. Father was barely able to restrain me from going after him. He pulled me back from the door and I was just able to see Friend running back towards the village, limping a little . . .

A childhood, when all is said and done, remains a childhood. A new situation brings new experiences, new problems and joys, and without ever forgetting all that happened to me on the shores of Baikal, my memories gradually began to lose their edge, and only if I found myself alone on a moonlit night would the crescent of the young moon cause me to return to the sadness of the past.

Many years went by.

My life has taken many different turnings and if it has not always been successful, it is perhaps because of a feeling which I have not yet understood myself: the feeling that the life I have lived has always been temporal and that, possibly, all my past was nothing other than a preparation for my return. For that reason I feel sure that one day I shall got to Irkutsk, board the train to Slyudyanka and sit on the left-hand side of the carriage; then, when the break in the mountains unveils the blue water and the brown crags, I shall discover for myself the essence of what is called the meaning of life.